ALSO BY RICHARD PAUL EVANS

A Winter Dream
Lost December
Promise Me
The Christmas List
Grace
The Gift
Finding Noel
The Sunflower
A Perfect Day
The Last Promise
The Christmas Box Miracle
The Carousel
The Looking Glass
The Locket
The Letter
Timepiece
The Christmas Box

The Walk Series
Miles to Go
The Road to Grace

For Young Adults
Michael Vey: The Prisoner of Cell 25
Michael Vey: Rise of the Elgen

THE

Walk

✶RICHARD PAUL EVANS✶

SIMON & SCHUSTER PAPERBACKS

NEW YORK   LONDON   TORONTO   SYDNEY   NEW DELHI

Simon & Schuster Paperbacks
A Divison of Simon & Schuster, Inc.
1230 Avenue of the Americas
New York, NY 10020

First Simon & Schuster trade paperback edition January 2013

SIMON & SCHUSTER PAPERBACKS and colophon are registered trademarks
of Simon & Schuster, Inc.

For information about special discounts for bulk purchases,
please contact Simon & Schuster Special Sales at
1-866-506-1949 or business@simonandschuster.com.

The Simon & Schuster Speakers Bureau can bring authors
to your live event. For more information or to book an event,
contact the Simon & Schuster Speakers Bureau at
1-866-248-3049 or visit our website at www.simonspeakers.com.

Designed by Davina Mock-Maniscalco

Manufactured in the United States of America

1   3   5   7   9   10   8   6   4   2

The Library of Congress has cataloged the hardcover edition as follows:
Evans, Richard Paul.
The walk / Richard Paul Evans.
        p.   cm.
1. Voyages and travels—Fiction.   2. Identity (Psychology)—Fiction.
3. Diary fiction.   I. Title.
PS3555.V259W35   2010
813'.54—dc22   2009052981
ISBN 978-1-4391-8731-9
ISBN 978-1-4391-9142-2 (pbk)
ISBN 978-1-4391-9990-9 (ebook)

✦ A C K N O W L E D G M E N T S ✦

oremost, I wish to thank my friend, Leo Thomas (Tom) Gandley, who lived more of this book than anyone would choose to. I know that it was oftentimes difficult to share the loss of your own "McKale," and I am grateful for your contribution to this book.

Also, Karen Christoffersen and her beloved Al. May his name live on around the world through these books.

I also wish to thank the usual suspects, with a few changes to the line-up. First of all my friend and former editor, Sydny Miner. It has been a pleasure working with you for more than a decade. I wish you well. Amanda, I look forward to walking on with you. Thanks for your help.

Acknowledgments

David Rosenthal and Carolyn Reidy for believing in the idea for this series.

Gypsy da Silva for enduring my impossible schedules with a smile. Liss, for being my advocate and friend. I love you.

Dr. Brent Mabey and Caitlin James for research assistance. The wonderful staff at the Redmond, Washington, Marriott, who set us on the right path.

Lisa Johnson, Barry Evans, Miche Barbosa, Diane Glad, Heather McVey, Judy Schiffman, Fran Platt, Lisa McDonald, Sherri Engar, Doug Smith, and Barbara Thompson.

My family: Keri, Jenna and David Welch, Allyson-Danica, Abigail, McKenna, and Michael. Jenna, thanks again for your help, love, and insight. Now get your own book done!

And, of course, my dear readers. Welcome to my walk.

—Richard

✴ To my father, David O. Evans ✴

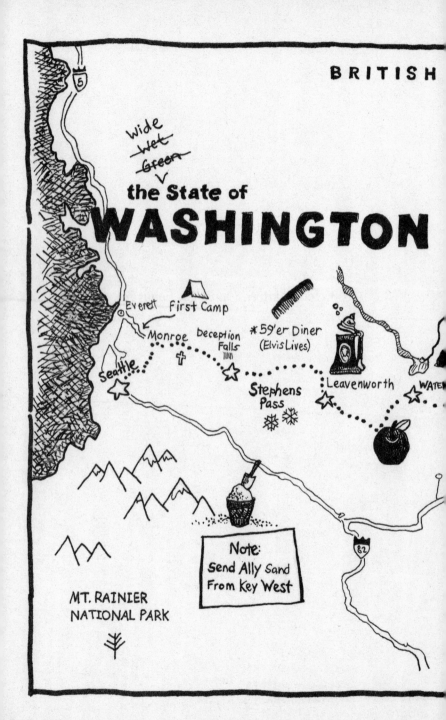

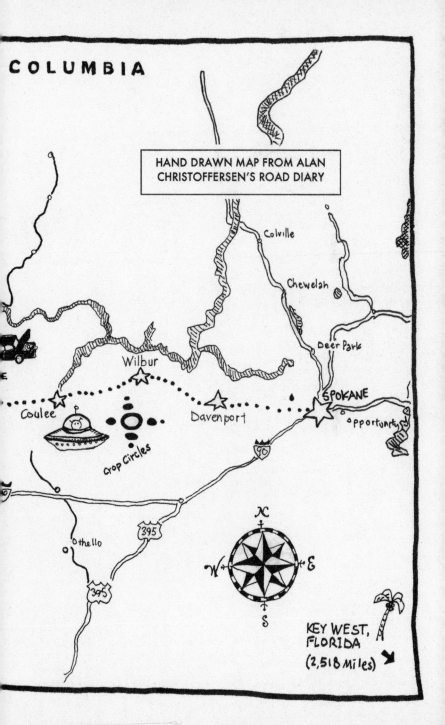

COLUMBIA

HAND DRAWN MAP FROM ALAN
CHRISTOFFERSEN'S ROAD DIARY

Colville

Chewelah

Deer Park

Wilbur

Coulee

Davenport

SPOKANE

opportunity

Crop Circles

90

Othello

395

395

N

W E

S

KEY WEST,
FLORIDA
(2,518 Miles)

THE Walk

PROLOGUE

Dear Alan,

As you write the story of your walk, I offer you some writing advice from one of your favorite authors, Lewis Carroll:

"Begin at the beginning and go on till you come to the end; then stop."

Alan Christoffersen's diary

My name is Alan Christoffersen. You don't know me. "Just another book in the library," my father would say. "Unopened and unread." You have no idea how far I've come or what I've lost. More important, you have no idea what I've found.

I'm no one important or famous. No matter. It is better to be loved by one person who knows your soul than millions who don't even know your phone number. I have loved and been loved as deeply as a man can hope for, which makes me a lucky man. It also means that I have suffered. Life has taught me that to fly, you must first accept the possibility of falling.

I don't know if anyone will ever read what I'm writing. But if you are holding this book, then you have found my story. You are now my fellow sojourner. If you find something in my journey that will help with yours, keep it.

Some might call this a love story. Those without love will call it a travelogue. To me, it is one man's journey to find hope. There are things that happened to me that you might not believe. There were lessons learned that you might not be ready for. No matter. Accept or dismiss what you will. But let me warn you in advance—which is more than I got—that what you read won't be easy. But it's a story worth telling. It's the story of my walk.

CHAPTER

One

"Above all, do not lose your desire to walk.
I know of no thought so burdensome that
one cannot walk away from it."

—Kierkegaard

Alan Christoffersen's diary

According to legend, once the sand of Key West is in your shoes, you cannot go back from whence you came. It is true for me. I'm alone on the beach watching the blood-red sun baptized in the Gulf of Mexico. And there is no returning to what I left behind.

The air is saturated with the smells of salt water and kelp and the sounds of breaking waves and screeching seagulls. Some part of me wonders if this might be a dream and hopes I'll wake in bed and find that I'm still in Seattle, and McKale is gently running her fingernails up and down my back. She would whisper, "Are you awake, my love?" I would turn to her and say, "You'll never believe what I just dreamed."

But it's no dream. I've walked the entire length of the country. And the woman I love is never coming back.

The water before me is as blue as windshield wiper fluid. I feel the twilight breeze against my unshaven, sunburned face, and I close my eyes. I've come a long way to get here—nearly 3,500 miles. But, in ways, I've come much further. Journeys cannot always be measured in physical distance.

I slide the backpack off my shoulders and sit down on the sand to untie my shoes and pull off my socks. My threadbare, once white, now-gray cotton socks stick to my feet as I peel them off. Then I step forward on the wet, shell-studded sand and wait for the receding water to return and cover my feet. I've had hundreds of hours to think about this moment, and I let it all roll over me: the wind, the water, the past and present, the world I left behind, the people and towns along the way. It's hard to believe I'm finally here.

After a few minutes, I go back and sit cross-legged in the sand next to my pack and do what I always do at the pivotal moments of my life: I take out a pen, open my diary, and begin to write.

My writing habit began long ago—long before this diary, long before my walk. The Christmas I was eight years old, my mother gave me my first diary. It was a small, yellow vinyl book debossed with deep flourishes. My favorite feature was its brass key and lock. It made me feel important to have something in my life of such consequence that I needed to lock it up from the world. That Christmas night was the first time in my life that I wrote in a diary. I figured with the lock and all, only I would be reading it, so I wrote the entry to myself, a habit I would continue the rest of my life.

The Walk

Dear Alan,

    Today is Christmas. I got a Rock'em Sockem Robots, a set of walky-talkys and red sweetish fish that I already ate. Mom gave me this diary with a lock and key and told me I should write every day. I asked her to write on my first page.

My Dear Son,

    Thank you for letting me write in your special book. And Merry Christmas! It is a very special Christmas. You will someday understand this. Every so often read these words and remember how much I love you and always will.

                                  —Mom

    Mom says it doesn't matter what I write and if I wait to write just the important things then I'll probly never write anything, because important things just look like everything else except when you look back on them. The thing is to write what yor thinking and feeling. Mom looked better today. I think she'll be better soon.

I've touched that writing so often that it's barely legible. My mother's entry was one of those events she spoke of, the kind that look like nothing except through time's rearview mirror. My mother died from breast cancer forty-nine days later—on Valentine's Day.

It was early in the morning, before I usually got up for school, that my father led me into the room to see her. On the nightstand next to her bed there was a single yellow rose in a bud vase and my homemade Valentine's card, with a drawing of a heart with an arrow through it. Her body was there, but she wasn't. She would have smiled and called to me. She would have praised my drawing. I knew she wasn't there.

In my father's typical stoic manner, we never spoke about her death. We never talked about feelings nor the things that gave rise to them. That morning he made me breakfast, then we sat at the table, listening to the silence. The people from the mortuary came and went, and my father managed everything with the steadiness of a business transaction. I'm not saying he didn't care. He just didn't know how to show his feelings. That was my father. I never once kissed him. That's just the way he was.

The reason we start things is rarely the reason we continue them.

Alan Christoffersen's Road Diary

I started writing in my diary because my mother told me to. After her death, I continued because to stop would be to break a chain that connected me to her. Then, gradually, even that changed. I didn't realize it at the time, but the reason I wrote was always changing. As I grew older, I wrote as proof of my existence. I write, there-fore *I am*.

I am. In each of us, there is something that, for better or worse, wants the world to know we existed. This is my story—my witness of myself and the greatest journey of my life. It began when I least expected it. At a time when I thought nothing could possibly go wrong.

CHAPTER

The garden of Eden is an archetype for all who have lost, which is the whole of humanity. To have is to lose, as to live is to die. Still, I envy Adam. For though he lost Eden, he still had his Eve.

Alan Christoffersen's diary

Before my world collapsed, I was a Seattle advertising executive, though, admittedly, that title rings a bit pretentious for someone who decorated his office with Aquaman figurines and Einstein posters. I was an *ad guy*. You could ask what got me into this line of business, but I really couldn't tell you. It's just something I always wanted to do. Maybe it was because I wanted to be Darrin on *Bewitched*. (I had a boyhood crush on Elizabeth Montgomery.) In 1998, I graduated from college in graphic design and landed a job before the ink on my diploma dried.

I thrived in the ad world and relished the life of a young rising star. A wunderkind. I won two ADDY's my first year and four the next. Then, after three years of making my bosses rich, I followed the preferred path of ad agencies, law firms, and organized religion and split off to form my own company. I was only twenty-eight years old when they pressed the name of my agency in vinyl lettering on my office door.

MADGIC
Advertising and Graphic Design

The company grew from two employees to a dozen in just nine weeks, and I was making more money than a Barbra Streisand ticket scalper. One of my clients proclaimed me a *poster boy for the American dream.* After two years, I had all the accoutrements of material success: my own business, a Lexus sports coupe, European vacations, and a beautiful, $1.9 million home in Bridle Trails—an exclusive, wooded neighborhood just north of Bellevue with an equestrian park and riding trails instead of sidewalks.

And, to complete this picture of success, I had a wife I adored—a brunette beauty named McKale. Potential clients would ask me if I could sell their products, and I would show them a picture of McKale and say, "I got her to marry me," and they would nod in astonishment and give me their business.

McKale was the love of my life and, literally, the girl next door. I met her when I had just turned nine, about four months after my mother died and my father moved us from Colorado to Arcadia, California.

It was late summer, and McKale was sitting alone in her front yard at a card table, selling Kool-Aid from a glass pitcher. She wore a short, above-the-knee skirt with pink cowboy boots. I asked her if I could help, and she looked me over for a moment then said, "No."

I ran upstairs to my bedroom and drew her a large, poster board–sized sign:

Kold Kool-Ade
Just 10¢

(I thought the K on *Kold* was a nice touch.) I went back down and presented my creation. She liked my sign enough to let me sit next to her. I suppose that's really why I got into advertising: to get the girl. We talked and drank Dixie cups of her black cherry elixir, which she still made me pay for. She was beautiful. She had perfect features: long, coffee-brown hair, freckles, and chocolate-syrup brown eyes that even an ad guy couldn't over hype. We ended up spending a lot of time together that summer. Actually, every summer from then on.

Like me, McKale had no siblings. And she too had been through tough times. Her parents divorced about two months before we moved in. As she told the story, it wasn't a usual divorce preceded by a lot of yelling and breaking of things. Her mother just up and left, leaving her alone with her father, Sam. McKale's mind was always processing what had gone wrong though, at times, she seemed stuck, like when a computer locks up and you sit there watching the hourglass, waiting for something to happen. It's a shame that humans don't come with reset buttons.

Our broken pieces fit together. We shared our deepest secrets, insecurities, fears, and, at times, our hearts. When I was ten, I started calling her Mickey. She liked that. It was the same year we built a tree house in her backyard. We spent a lot of time in it. We played board games, like Mouse Trap and Sorry, and we even had sleepovers. On her eleventh birthday, I found her there sitting in the corner, crying hysterically. When she could speak, she said,

"How could she leave me? How could a mother just do that?" She wiped her eyes angrily.

I couldn't answer her. I had wondered the same thing.

"You're lucky your mother died," she said.

I didn't like that. "I'm lucky my mother died?"

Between sobs she said, "Your mother would have stayed if she could. My mother chose to leave me. She's still out there somewhere. I wish she had died instead."

I sat down next to her and put my arm around her. "I'll never leave you."

She laid her head on my shoulder. "I know."

McKale was my guide to the female world. One time she wanted to kiss just to see what the big deal was. We kissed for about five minutes. I liked it. A lot. I'm not so sure she did because she never asked to do it again, so we didn't.

That was the way it was with us. If McKale didn't like something, we didn't do it. I could never figure out why she always got to make the rules, but I always followed them. I eventually decided that's just how things were.

She was very frank about growing up a girl. Sometimes I'd ask her things, and she'd say, "I don't know. This is new to me too."

When she was thirteen, I asked her why she didn't have girlfriends.

She answered as if she'd given it a lot of thought. "I don't like girls."

"Why?"

"I don't trust them." Then she added, "I like horses."

McKale went horseback riding just about every week.

Every month or so, she invited me to come, but I always told her I was busy. The truth was that I was terrified of horses. Once, when I was seven, Dad, Mom, and I took a summer vacation to a dude ranch in Wyoming called Juanita Hot Springs. On our second day, we went on a horseback ride. My horse was a paint named Cherokee. I had never been on a horse before, so I held onto the leather saddle horn with one hand and the reins with the other, hating every moment of it. During the ride, some of the cowboys decided to race, and my horse decided to join them. When he bolted, I dropped the reins and clung to the horn, screaming for help. Fortunately, one of the cowboys turned back to rescue me, though he couldn't hide his contempt for my "city boy" ways. All he said was, "I been riding since I was three." Not surprisingly, I never shared McKale's love of horses.

Horses aside, we were almost always together, from elementary school through the awkward ages, including the middle-school years—the armpit of life. At the age of fifteen, McKale physically matured, and high school boys started buzzing around her house like yellow jackets at a barbecue. Of course, I noticed the change in her too, and it drove me crazy. You're not supposed to have those kinds of feelings about your best friend.

I was purple with jealousy. I didn't have a chance against those guys. They had mustaches. I had acne. They had muscle cars. I had a bus pass. I was remarkably uncool.

McKale's father's parenting style was best described as laissez-faire, and when he let her date in junior high, she could barely keep track of her own social schedule. After her dates she would come over to my house to debrief, which was a little like describing the buffet meal you just ate to a starving man. I remember after one of her dates she asked, "Why do men always want to possess you?"

I shook my head. "I don't know," I replied, wanting to possess her more than anything in the world.

Her situation with boys was like a baseball game: someone was always up to bat, someone on deck, and a couple dozen guys waiting in the dugout, every one of them hoping to round the bases with my best friend. I felt more like a hot dog vendor in the stands than one of the players.

Sometimes she would ask my advice about a particular guy, and I would give her a remarkably self-serving answer, and she would just look at me with a funny expression. I was miserable. She once said that since I was her best friend, when she got married I'd have to be her bridesmaid, which meant I'd have to shave my legs, and how did I feel about chiffon? I don't know if she was purposely torturing me or if it just came naturally.

At sixteen things changed. I had a growth spurt, and the opposite sex took a sudden interest in me. This had an interesting effect on McKale. While she had relished sharing every excruciating detail of her dates, she never wanted to hear about mine. She initiated a "don't ask, don't tell" policy. I remember one fall afternoon, two girls came over to see me while McKale and I were talking on the front porch of her house. They sidled over and joined us. One of them had a thing for me, and both were laying the flirt on pretty heavy. McKale stormed inside, slamming the door behind her.

"What's her prob?" one of the girls asked.

"Jealous," the other said. I remember feeling a warm rush of hope.

Still, if she had romantic feelings for me, she hid them well, and for the most part, I suffered in silence. And for good reason. McKale was my best friend, and there's no better way to ruin a friendship than to declare your love to an unreceptive recipient. Fortunately I never had to.

One warm June day—it was my seventeenth birthday—we were on the hammock in her backyard, lying opposite each other, her tiny, bare feet next to my shoulder. We were gently rocking back and forth, arguing about where the Beatles would be if it weren't for Yoko when she suddenly said, "You know *we're* going to get married someday."

I don't know where this news came from—I just remember an impossibly large smile crossing my face. I tried to act cool. "You think?"

"I know."

"How do you know?"

"Because you're so madly in love with me you can't stand it."

It seemed pointless to deny it. "You noticed?"

"Yeah," she said matter of factly. "Everyone notices. The mailman noticed."

I felt stupid.

Her voice softened, "And the thing is . . . I feel the same way about you."

She swung her legs over the side and sat up, bringing her face close to mine. I looked up at her, and she was staring at me with wet eyes. "You know I love you, don't you? I could never live without you."

I probably felt the same way a lottery winner feels when their number is read. At that moment, a friendship of seven years disappeared into something else. We kissed, and this time I could tell she liked it. It was to be the second greatest day of my life. Our wedding day was my first.

There's a problem with marrying up. You always worry that someday they'll see through you and leave. Or, worse yet, someone better will come along and take her. In my case, it wasn't someone. And it wasn't something better.

CHAPTER

Three

The assumption of time is one of humanity's greatest follies. We tell ourselves that there's always tomorrow, when we can no more predict tomorrow than we can the weather. Procrastination is the thief of dreams.

Alan Christoffersen's diary

McKale and I married young, though it didn't seem young at the time. Probably because I felt I had been waiting my whole life and wanted to get on with it. We got an apartment in Pasadena, just three miles from where we grew up. McKale got a job as a legal secretary for a small-time lawyer, and I went to school at the Art Center College of Design, just a bus ride away from our home.

Those were good years. We had our arguments—all marriages require adjustments—but they never really lasted. How can you hurt a person you love more than yourself? It's like punching yourself in the head. I got good at apologizing, though she usually beat me to it. Sometimes I suspected that we really just fought so we could have fun making up.

The thing we argued most about was children. McKale wanted to start a family right away. I was against the idea, and because logistics and finances seemed to be on my side, it was an argument I always won. "At least wait until I'm out of school," I said.

As soon as I had graduated from college and landed my first steady job, McKale brought up the subject again, but again I told her that I wasn't ready. I wanted to wait until life was more *secure*. What a fool I was.

⋆

I worked at Conan Cross Advertising for about three years
before I decided to hang out my own shingle in October
of 2005. That same week, I started a city-wide billboard
campaign to promote myself. The billboard read:

AL CHRISTOFFERSEN IS A MADMAN.

The board created a small stir locally, and I even got a
call from a lawyer threatening to sue me on behalf of his
client, with whom I shared the same name. After three
weeks I made a few changes to the sign. It now read:

AL CHRISTOFFERSEN IS Aɴ MADMAN
(Call Al for some sane advertising advice.)

The campaign won me another ADDY and brought
in three very large clients. If I thought my previous em-
ployer ran a sweatshop, it was an afternoon tea party compared to being self-employed. I'd spend all day pitching
and meeting with clients and most evenings producing
the work. Several times a week, McKale brought dinner
down to the office. We'd sit on the floor of my office and
eat Chinese takeout and catch up on each other's day.

As my agency grew, it became clear that I needed help.
One day it walked into my office. Kyle Craig, a man with
two first names, was a former rep for the local television
station. I had purchased time on his station, and he had
been following my agency's meteoric rise. He made me

an offer: for a salary and 15 percent of the company, he'd take over client relations and media buying so I could focus on marketing and advertising creation. It was exactly what I needed.

Kyle was well dressed, ambitious, and charming: a consummate salesman. He was the kind of guy who could talk a nun into the cigar-of-the-month club.

McKale didn't really like Kyle. She didn't trust him. She told me that the first time they met, he had flirted with her. I shrugged it off. "He just comes across that way," I said. "He's harmless." Truth was, I liked Kyle. We were rogue ad guys—young, smarmy, slick-talking boys who worked hard and *had fun* doing it. Back then there was a lot of fun to be had.

One of those times was when the suits at the Seattle county commissioner's office asked us to prepare an advertising proposal for their chronically un-hip county fair. The year before, there had been a gang-related shooting at the fair, and attendance and profits had fallen through the floor. They predicted that this year would be even worse. The director of county services heard we were good and invited us to pitch their account. I created a hilarious campaign with talking cows. (That was before California Cheese Association's HAPPY COW campaigns. You could say I was into talking cows before talking cows were cool.)

Neither Kyle nor I had ever met the people we were pitching, and so, to break the ice, I thought we'd have some fun by presenting a prank billboard campaign. In the history of bad ideas, this was the equivalent of a concrete parachute. I failed to take into account that bureaucrats don't have a sense of humor.

The temperature dropped a few degrees as the fair's marketing committee entered our office. There were three of them, rigid and gray—so tightly wound I expected their heads to start spinning.

I didn't know their names so I created my own for them: Hat Guy, Church Lady, and Captain High Pants. They sat at our conference room table and looked at me expectantly. I've attended funerals that were less solemn. Unwisely, I stuck to my plan and presented the first prank board.

Come to the fair,
The GANG'S all here

They stared at the sign in stunned disbelief.

"Gangs . . . ," Church Lady squeaked.

"Here's the next one," I said. Kyle's eyes were practically bulging.

Show your TRUE COLORS
attend the county fair

No one spoke for a moment, then Hat Guy said, "Colors? Like gang colors?"

Without answering him I revealed the next slide.

Have a KILLER Time
at the county fair

Their three, trout-like mouths simultaneously fell open, and Church Lady gasped. Captain High Pants looked down for a moment and adjusted his glasses. "I think we've come to the wrong place."

Kyle jumped to his feet. "Hey, we're just pulling your chain," he said. "Having a little fun."

"That's right," I said. "I just thought we'd lighten things up with a little humor."

Captain High Pants looked at Kyle with the cold stare of an immigration officer. "This is your idea of humor?"

Kyle pointed at me. "Actually, it's *his* idea of humor."

"I don't find it very amusing," Church Lady said, standing.

They gathered their things and walked out of the room, leaving Kyle and me looking at each other in astonishment.

"That went well," Kyle said.

"Think they'll come back?" I asked.

"Nope."

"Yeah, me neither," I said.

"Bunch of cow-lovers," Kyle said. "I hope the Crips stage a shoot-out in their hog exhibit this year."

(Note: The agency they eventually selected produced the most boring campaign I'd ever seen, which fit them nicely: a television campaign with two old biddies who looked like Mayberry's Aunt Bea, sipping iced tea and talking about the good ole days when the Fair came to town.)

CHAPTER

Four

Often the simplest of decisions carry the divest of consequences.

Alan Christoffersen's diary

The beginning of the collapse came on a day like any other. The alarm went off at six, and I reached over and hit the snooze button. McKale nuzzled up to me, pressing her soft, warm body against mine. She began gently running her nails up and down my chest, one of my favorite things in the world. I exhaled in ecstasy. "Don't stop."

She kissed my neck. "What are you doing today?"

"Work."

"Call in sick."

"It's our company. Who would I call in sick to?"

"You can call me. I'll give you time off."

"For good behavior?"

"No. You're not good at all."

I smiled and kissed her. Every morning I woke up amazed that this woman was still in my bed.

"I wish I could. But we're pitching the Wathen account today."

"Isn't that why you have Kyle? Can't he handle these things?"

"Not today. This is the *big* one I've been preparing for all month. I have to be there."

"You're no fun."

"Someone's got to pay the bills."

Her expression changed. She lay back. "Speaking of which . . ."

I rolled over. "What?"

"I need more money."

"Again?"

"I haven't made the house payment yet."

"For this month or last month?"

She grimaced. ". . . last month."

"McKale." I groaned in exasperation. "I got a call at the office last week from the leasing company. They said we missed the last two months' payments."

"I know. I'll get to it. I hate handling the money. I'm no good at money."

"You're good at spending it."

She frowned. "That was mean."

I looked at her and my expression softened. "Sorry. You know you're the reason I earn it."

She leaned forward and kissed me. "I love you."

"I love you too," I said. "I'll have Steve transfer some money into your account." I sat up. "We may be celebrating tonight. Or not. Either way let's do something fun. We have the whole weekend."

She got a big smile. "I have an idea."

"What?"

"I'm not going to tell you." She put her finger on my lips. "I guarantee you'll never forget this weekend."

Neither of us could have guessed how right she was.

CHAPTER

Humans waste far too much time worrying about things that will never befall them. It's my experience that the greatest tragedies are the ones that don't even cross our minds—the events that blindside us on a Friday afternoon when we're wondering how to spend our weekend.

Or when we're in the middle of an advertising pitch.

I pulled into my private parking stall about twenty minutes after nine. Kyle was already in a bad mood. "Glad you could make it," he said, as I walked into the office. I was used to this. Kyle was always uptight before a big presentation.

"Relax, Kyle," I said calmly.

Falene walked in behind Kyle. "Good morning, Alan."

"Morning, Falene."

Falene was my girl Friday—a sleek, olive-skinned beauty of Greek descent whom Kyle had met on a model search and hired as our executive assistant and resident eye candy. Even her name (her mother had given birth the night she saw *Bambi*) was exotic.

"Relax?" Kyle said, his voice strained. "This is the Super Bowl. You don't show up late on game day."

I kept walking toward my office followed by Kyle and Falene. "Are they here yet?"

"No."

"Then I'm not late."

"Can I get you anything before the meeting?" Falene asked.

"How about a sedative for Kyle?" I said.

Falene smiled wryly. Even though Kyle had hired her, she had never been crazy about him. Lately the relationship seemed worse.

"I'll meet you in the conference room," Kyle grumbled.

I understood why Kyle was so anxious. The client we were about to pitch was Wathen Development Company and the campaign was for an upscale housing development called The Bridge: a $200 million project, with 400 units, two clubhouses, and an 18-hole golf course. Their annual advertising budget exceeded $3 million.

Wathen, a brash, perennially tan forty-something developer, arrived about fifteen minutes later. He was flanked by his accountant, Stuart, and Abby, a British woman we'd never met and whose role was unclear. Kyle and I shook hands with them as they entered our office.

"What can we get you to drink?" Kyle asked.

"What have you got?"

"What's on tap, Falene?" Kyle asked curtly. Falene glared at him, then turned to Wathen.

"Mr. Wathen," she said, "we have . . ."

"Call me Phil."

Falene smiled. "Okay, Phil. We have juice: cranberry, apple, pineapple, and orange. We have seltzers, vanilla and peach, and Coke, Diet Coke, Pepsi, Perrier . . ."

"They still make that Perrier?"

"I'm afraid so."

He laughed. "I'll have a cranberry juice. Could you mix a little pineapple in with that?"

"Certainly."

"Abby," Wathen said, "what'll you have?"

"Nothing."

"I'll have a vanilla seltzer," Stuart said.

"Very well," Falene said. "I'll be right back with your drinks."

As Falene walked out, Kyle invited everyone into the conference room. As we were settling in around the table, something peculiar happened—something a little difficult to explain. I suddenly felt a sharp pain up my spine, followed by a powerful emotional flux, a bizarre feeling of oppression that seemed to press the very breath from me. At first I wondered if I was having a heart attack or a stroke, then an anxiety attack. Whatever it was, it passed as quickly as it came. No one seemed to notice that I was breathing heavy.

I had designed the conference room to showcase my myriad awards. The walls were textured with plaster then painted aubergine and covered with gold-framed advertising awards. The south wall had two crowded shelves that held our trophies. The awards on the east wall were concealed behind a screen that descended from the ceiling.

When everyone was situated around the table, I turned on the room's projector, and the Wathen Development logo appeared on the screen.

Falene returned, careful to take the first drink to Wathen. "There you are, sir, I mean, Phil. Cranberry with a splash of pineapple. Anything else?"

"Just to be twenty again," he said.

Abby rolled her eyes.

She distributed the rest of the drinks, including a Coke to Kyle, which, I noticed, she did without looking at him.

"All right," Kyle said, "if it's all right with you, Phil, we'll begin." Wathen nodded, and Kyle dimmed the lights with a hand remote. "Thank you for this opportunity. Our objective, as your future agency, is to create a campaign that will not only result in capacity occupancy of your new development, but a demand that will keep your real estate value strong and growing.

"Our campaign employs a multimedia approach that includes television, radio, newspaper, Internet, and outdoor advertising. We propose to launch the campaign with a fifty-billboard showing with the express purpose of creating name awareness. We'll accomplish this with a three-phase outdoor message, the first to begin as soon as you're ready to pull the trigger." He pointed to me. "Al . . ."

I pressed a button on the remote to unveil the first billboard comp.

Bridge under construction

The board was yellow and black like a road hazard sign. Kyle and I simultaneously glanced at Wathen. He showed no emotion. His lack of response made Kyle visibly nervous. "It's a teaser campaign," Kyle said. "We'd run this with both a south and north exposure on I-5 and I-45 for two months."

"It looks like a detour sign," Abby said.

"Exactly," I replied.

She continued. "But what if people think that some bridge is really under construction?"

"Actually, that's our hope," I replied. "These potential clients of yours drive past several hundred billboards every day. They've learned to tune all those signs out, but not the directional signs. As they discover they've been tricked, this will give them a relationship with your development. After thirty days, we unveil the second board." I pressed a button.

Bridge opens July 16th

"This is when we begin the television and radio campaign," Kyle said. "While up to this point the campaign image has been purposely austere, the campaign now begins to show a luxurious aspect: upscale, beautiful, chic, happy people enjoying the exclusive lifestyle and amenities of The Bridge. You'll notice that the bright yellow of the first board has subtly changed to a tint more gold."

"And then," I said, "with the opening of Phase I, the final board."

The Bridge is now open.
Cross over to Washington's premier new Lifestyle

Wathen smiled and slightly nodded. Stuart leaned over to whisper something to Wathen, and Abby was also smiling.

Just then Falene opened the door. In a terse whisper she said my name, "Al."

Kyle looked at her incredulously. She knew better than to interrupt at such a crucial moment. I gave her a quick headshake. She walked to my side and crouched down next to me. "Alan, it's an emergency. McKale's had an accident."

"What kind of accident?" I said loud enough that everyone looked at me.

"Your neighbor's on the line. She says it's serious."

I stood. "I'm sorry, my wife's been in an accident. I need to take this call."

"Go ahead and take it here," Wathen said, motioning to the phone in the middle of the table.

Falene turned up the lights. I lifted the receiver and pushed down on the flashing button. "This is Al."

"Alan this is your neighbor, Monnie Olsen. McKale's been in an accident."

My heart froze. "What kind of accident?"

"She was thrown from her horse."

"How bad is she hurt?"

"She was rushed to Overland."

Everything in my mind was swimming. "How bad is it? Tell me."

She hesitated then suddenly began to cry. "They think she's broken her back." Her voice faltered. "She . . ." she stopped. "I'm sorry, she said she couldn't feel anything below her waist. You need to get to Overland."

"I'm on my way." I hung up the phone.

"Is she okay?" Wathen asked.

"No. It's bad. I've got to go."

"I'll finish up," Kyle said.

As I left the room, Falene put her hand on my back. "What do you need?"

"Prayers. Lots of prayers."

✦

I sped to the hospital, oblivious to the world around me. The drive seemed endless, and the whole way there an adrenaline-fueled dialogue took place in my head—a battle between two polar forces. The first voice assured me that my neighbor was just panicked and everything was fine. Then another voice shouted, *It's worse than they're saying. It's bad beyond your worst nightmare.*

By the time I reached the hospital I was nearly crazed with fear. I parked in a handicap zone outside the emergency entrance and ran inside and up to the first admittance window, where a middle-aged woman with thick glasses sat behind a glass partition. She was looking at her computer screen and didn't notice me.

I tapped on the glass. "My wife's in here," I said frantically.

She looked up at me.

"McKale Christoffersen. I'm her husband."

She typed the name into her computer. "Oh, yes. Just a minute." She picked up her phone and dialed a number. She spoke softly to someone then hung up and turned back. "We have someone coming to speak with you. Have a seat, please."

I sat down in a chair and covered my eyes with my hand and rocked back and forth. I don't know how long I had been like that when I felt a hand on my shoulder and looked up. It was our neighbors, Monnie and Tex Olsen. The moment I saw their stricken faces something burst inside me. I began sobbing. Monnie put her arms around me. "We're so sorry."

"Have you talked with the doctors?" Tex asked.

I shook my head. "They're still with her." I turned to Monnie, "Did you see it happen?"

She knelt down beside me and spoke quietly. "No, I found her just a few minutes after it happened. Her horse got spooked and threw her."

"How was she?"

I wanted to hear comforting words, but she just shook her head. "Not good."

It was another ten minutes before a young woman, boyish-faced with short hair, slacks, and a silk blouse with a plastic name tag hanging from a lanyard around her neck walked out of the double-doored ER into the waiting room. The woman behind the glass motioned to me, though I'm sure it was only for confirmation. It wasn't hard to pick out the guy in distress. "Mr. Christoffersen?"

I stood. "Yes."

"I'm Shelly Crandall. I'm a hospital social worker."

They sent a social worker? I thought. "I want to see my wife."

"I'm sorry, but the doctors are still working on her."

"What's going on?"

"Your wife has had a spinal fracture in her upper back. The doctors are stabilizing her."

"Is she paralyzed?" The words sprang from my mouth.

She hesitated. "It's too soon to say. In an injury like this there's a lot of swelling, and that can affect the nerves. We usually wait seventy-two hours for an accurate prognosis of the damage to the spinal cord."

"When can I see her?"

"It will still be a few hours. I promise, I'll take you to her as soon as she's out. I'm sorry, Mr. Christoffersen."

I slumped back down in the chair. Monnie and her husband sat across from me, silent.

The wait was excruciating. Every minute that the clock ticked off seemed to steal hope with it. I listened anxiously to the overhead announcements about incoming traumas and patient emergencies, wondering if they were talking about McKale.

Almost two hours after I arrived, the social worker led me back through the double doors of the ER. My first thought when I saw my wife was that there had been a mistake, and they'd taken me to the wrong room. McKale was vibrant and strong. The woman lying in the bed in a hospital gown looked tiny and fragile. Broken.

My McKale was broken. Her eyes were closed, and her hair was spread out on the pillow behind her. The bed was flanked by monitors. There was an IV running from her right arm. I was surprised to see there was still dirt on her face. McKale had fallen face-first from the horse, and in the emergency effort, no one had taken the time to clean her off.

My legs felt as if my body suddenly weighed a ton. I leaned against the bedrail as my eyes filled with tears. "Mickey . . ."

At the sound of my voice, McKale's eyes fluttered, and she looked up at me.

I squeezed her hand. "I'm here."

Tears filled her eyes. Her voice came softly. "I'm so sorry."

I fought back my own tears. I needed to be strong for her. "What are you sorry for?"

"I ruined everything."

"No, baby. You're going to be okay. Everything's going to be okay."

She looked at me for a moment then closed her eyes. "No, it's not."

The next twenty-four hours passed like a nightmare. McKale's IV fed her a steady stream of morphine, and she dozed in and out of consciousness as I sat beside her. Once she woke and asked if this were a dream. How I wished I could have told her "yes." Around eight, I went out of the room to make some calls.

My first call was to McKale's father. He began to cry and promised he'd be out on the next available flight. Then I called my father. He was quiet when I told him. "I'm sorry, son. Do you need anything?"

"A miracle."

"Wish I had one. Do you need me to come up?"

"No."

"Okay." He was perfectly fine with that. We both were. That's just the way it was.

Later that night I got a call from Kyle. "How's McKale?"

"Just a minute," I said. I walked out of McKale's room.

"Her back's broken. It's bad. We just don't know how bad yet."

"But she's not paralyzed . . ."

I hated that word. "We don't know yet, but she can't move her legs."

He groaned. "There's hope, isn't there? Miracles happen every day."

"That's what we're hoping for."

We were both quiet for a long time. Then he said, "I called to tell you we got the Bridge account."

It took a minute for what he said to register. I was astonished that what had completely dominated my thoughts for weeks before no longer owned space or importance. Had it been another day, we would have been celebrating with an expensive meal and a bottle of champagne at Canlis. That world already seemed like a distant memory. All I said was, "Oh." I realized just how disconnected I'd suddenly become.

There was another long silence. Finally Kyle said, "Hey, don't worry about a thing, I've got everything under control."

"Thank you."

"Don't mention it. Did McKale get the flowers I sent?"

"Yes. Thank you."

"Give McKale my love. And don't worry, I've got your back."

CHAPTER

Six

Nothing is more excruciating than waiting
for the jury's verdict. Except, perhaps,
hearing the jury's verdict.

Alan Christoffersen's diary

The next three days ticked by in a surreal limbo, my heart vacillating between hope and despair. The doctors echoed what the social worker had said—they wouldn't know for certain the extent of the nerve damage for seventy-two hours. *A lot can happen in seventy-two hours*, I told myself. Maybe when the swelling decreased, she would get feeling and movement back.

She had to recover. McKale in bed, immobile, was about the most unnatural thing I could imagine.

The rest of my world ceased to exist. I stayed by McKale's side, and at night I slept in a cot next to her bed, at least tried to, since the nurses seemed to come in every twenty minutes to check on something. I didn't want her to wake and not have me there. McKale's father, Sam, arrived Saturday afternoon, and for the first time I left her side and went home to shower and change my clothes. I was only gone for a couple of hours.

Monday morning I didn't go home. It had been seventy-two hours since the accident, and the doctors had told us they were coming in the morning for her tests. Finally we were going to find out the extent of the damage. Sam arrived around ten. That morning none of us spoke of the tests. McKale talked to her father about his new home in Florida, then she asked me about work.

I realized then that I hadn't told her about the Bridge account.

"That's good news," she said.

Sam was more excited than both of us. "Well done, my boy. Well done."

I feigned a smile. I had no real interest in it and spoke of it only to take our minds from weightier matters.

Around eleven thirty, three doctors entered the room. One of them carried a small vinyl satchel, another a clipboard. I recognized the female doctor from the day of the accident. She said to me, "I'm Dr. Hardman. You're McKale's husband?"

"Yes, ma'am."

"And you're her father?"

Sam nodded.

"I'm going to need you both to leave while we conduct these tests."

I wanted to ask why but didn't. I put a lot of faith in the doctors. I realized later that it wasn't them I put faith in; it was my hope that she would be healed. Sam stepped away, and one of the doctors began pulling the curtains around the bed.

"May we stand outside and listen?" I asked, pointing to the other side of the curtain.

"Sure," she said.

I leaned over and kissed McKale's forehead. "I love you."

"I love you too."

I parted the curtain and walked outside next to Sam.

"How are you, McKale?" Dr. Hardman asked.

McKale mumbled something.

"I'm sorry. We're going to run some tests. They're quite simple. They shouldn't be painful." There was some shuffling, and McKale moaned in pain as they rolled her over to get a look at her spine.

I heard a bag unzipping, and then one of the doctors said, "Dr. Schiffman will touch various parts of your body with this tool." (After the procedure I saw *the tool*. It looked like a medieval torture device. It was shaped like a wheel, with pins radiating out from the center.) "We will run this along different parts of your body and then ask for a response. Are you ready?"

"Yes," McKale said meekly.

Then I heard one of the doctors ask, "Can you feel this, McKale?"

"Yes."

My heart thrilled. I wanted to high-five Sam, but he was just looking at the floor.

"Okay. Now we'll try below your waist. Can you feel this?"

There was a long pause. McKale said, "No."

"How about this?"

There was another pause. This time her voice was slightly strained. "No."

My stomach twisted. *C'mon, McKale.*

"How about this?"

McKale started to cry. "No."

I started silently praying. *Please, God. Let her feel something.*

"How about this?"

McKale was crying now. "No."

Sam put his hand over his eyes.

"And this?"

"No. I can't feel anything," she shouted. "I can't feel anything!"

I parted the curtain, but Dr. Hardman just shook her head at me. I stepped back.

"Now we're going to test for deep nerve damage. Sometimes nerve damage is just on the surface, and patients retain feeling under their skin. I am going to insert this needle into your leg, and I need you to tell me if you feel anything."

I kept waiting for something, but McKale didn't make a sound.

I dropped down to a chair and held my head in my hands. I felt sick. She had no feeling. McKale was paralyzed.

CHAPTER

Seven

As a boy I heard this story in church. A man was patching a pitched roof of a tall building when he began sliding off. As he neared the edge of the roof he prayed, "Save me, Lord, and I'll go to church every Sunday, I'll give up drinking, I'll be the best man this city has ever known."

As he finished his prayer, a nail snagged onto his overalls and saved him. The man looked up to the sky and shouted, "Never mind, God. I took care of it myself."

How true of us.

Alan Christoffersen's diary

In spite of the permanent damage to her nerves, her spine still needed to be repaired and she had to go back in for surgery. We had to wait another 24 hours before the hospital was able to fit her in. Sam had to fly home that morning, so I was the only one at McKale's side when they rolled her off to surgery. I waited tensely in the waiting room.

When the surgeon came out to give me an update, he had a large smile on his face. "That went very well. Even better than we expected. We were able to repair her spine without any major problems."

His tone elevated me. "Does that mean she might walk again?"

His expression fell. "No. It just means that the bones of the spine are repaired."

I'm told that there's a universal pattern to grief and loss that everyone must pass through. The first three stages are denial, anger, and bargaining. I suppose I did them all at once. I promised God everything. I'd give all my money to the poor, spend my life building homes for the homeless, anything that might get His attention.

I even had a plan for God to make it happen. I would just wake like the whole thing had been a bad dream. No one would even have to know what had happened. But I never woke from this dream. God had other plans.

CHAPTER

Eight

We are such fools. We punish our friends
and reward our enemies far more often
than we are willing to believe.

Alan Christoffersen's diary

Wednesday afternoon, Falene called. I didn't really want to take her call but did anyway. She had already called several times over the last week and left messages that she urgently needed to talk to me. She was surprised to hear my voice. "Alan?"

"Hi, Falene."

"How is McKale?"

"The damage to her nerves is permanent."

Falene slightly gasped. When she spoke, there was emotion in her voice. "I'm so sorry." After a few moments, she said, "What can I do?"

"There's nothing anyone can do," I said angrily. "If there were, we would have done it." Falene was silent. After a moment I said, "I'm sorry. I'm not doing well."

"I understand."

"What did you need to talk to me about?"

She hesitated. "It can wait," she said. "Things will work out. Give McKale my love."

I puzzled over her comment but pushed it aside. "All right, we'll talk later."

Kyle called later that evening. "How is McKale?"

"She's paralyzed."

Kyle was quiet for a moment. "I'm sorry, man. I wish there was something I could do."

I sniffed. "Yeah."

"I met with Wathen this morning. He asked how you're doing."

"Tell him thank you. And thank you for the flowers."

"Will do. He wanted to know when they could see some final graphics, so I put Ralph on it. Also, you have the studio scheduled for Tuesday's Coiffeur shoot. Have you selected a model?"

I ran my fingers through my hair. "No. I scheduled a model search for Thursday."

"Thursday, as in tomorrow?"

I had no idea what day it was. "Sorry. Can you handle that?"

"I'm always up for a model search."

I exhaled. "I'm sorry to drop all this on you, Kyle. I just can't go back to that world."

"You don't need to worry about a thing. I'll take care of everyone. By the way, has Falene called recently?"

"This afternoon."

He paused. "What did she say?"

"Not much. She just asked how McKale was."

"Oh?" He sounded surprised. "Good. That's good. Well, I better let you go. Give McKale my love."

"Thank you, Kyle."

"My pleasure."

CHAPTER

Nine

The more someone assures you that everything is okay, the more you can be assured that it's not.

Alan Christoffersen's diary

The next day McKale was released from the ICU and transferred to the rehabilitation wing of the hospital. I spent the next three weeks at McKale's side. I stayed until she fell asleep every night. One night I was so exhausted, I started to leave before she was asleep, and she begged me to stay. She was afraid, and she clung to me like a man clings to a limb at the edge of a waterfall. Maybe for the same reason.

I hated rehabilitation. I hated the name of the place. It was false advertising. Nothing was being rehabilitated. I don't think it was meant to do anything other than get McKale used to a life in a wheelchair, which proved more difficult than we hoped since she lacked the upper body strength to do much of what was required.

In addition to the physical therapy there was "emotional support" as well. A slew of counselors spewed out more promises than a late-night infomercial. *You can do anything, mountains just lift us higher, you can live a normal life, your life can be just as full as it was before, rah, rah, rah.*

McKale called it a "sorry excuse for a pep rally."

She wasn't buying any of it.

✦

Those first weeks after the accident, the only calls I received from the office, outside of those from Kyle and Falene, were repeated calls from two of my clients, Wathen and Coiffeur. Every time they called, I texted Kyle and asked him to take care of them. I just couldn't live in two worlds. Still, as much as I appreciated Kyle's covering for me, I knew it couldn't go on much longer.

By the end of the third week, as I made arrangements to bring McKale home, I began to prepare myself mentally to return to work. I called Kyle for an update on our accounts and was surprised when he didn't answer his cell phone. This went on for the next three days. By the end of the week, I wondered if he'd lost his phone. Friday afternoon I called Tawna, our receptionist, to find out where he was.

"Madgic, Falene speaking."

"What are you doing answering the phones?" I asked. "Where's Tawna?"

"She's gone."

"She left early?"

"No, she quit. Everyone's quit except me."

She might as well have been speaking Chinese for all the sense it made to me. "Quit? What are you talking about?"

"Kyle and Ralph started their own company. They took everyone with them."

I was stunned. "Kyle and Ralph left?"

"He and Ralph started their own agency. Craig/Jordan Advertising."

"What about our clients?"

"They've taken them all. Kyle told them Madgic was going under," she said angrily. "I did the best I could to save them. I convinced Wathen and Claudia at Coiffeur to call you first, but they said you wouldn't return their calls."

"We lost them all?"

"Every one."

I rubbed my face with my hand. "I can't believe it."

"I don't want to believe it. Tell me what to do."

My head felt as if it would explode. "I don't know, Falene. Just hang tight. McKale comes home Saturday. We'll get together Monday morning and strategize. How are we for money?"

"I called Steve about payroll. He said we're about out."

"That can't be. We should have received everyone's monthly retainers."

"I just know what he told me."

"Kyle," I said, thinking aloud. "He must have had them pay him their retainers."

"Can't you sue him?"

"He won't get away with this."

Falene sighed. "I'm sorry, Al. I know you didn't need this on top of everything else."

"We'll weather this, Falene. We'll talk Monday and make a plan."

Her voice calmed. "Okay. Give McKale my love."

"Falene."

"Yes."

"Thank you for not leaving."

"You're welcome. Besides, there's not enough money in the world to make me work for that creep."

CHAPTER

What never ceases to amaze me is the human capacity for self-deception when looking after one's own interest. Self-interest is blind.

Alan Christoffersen's diary

I must have called Kyle at least twenty times before he finally answered my call.

"Alan." He answered cheerfully, but his voice was tinged with anxiety.

"What have you done?"

"Why don't you tell me what you think I've done."

"You stole my agency." I had been sitting in an empty patients' lounge and now rose to my feet and started to pace.

"Not true, buddy. Madgic is still yours. I just followed in your path and struck out on my own."

"With *my* clients."

"No, with *my* clients. Don't forget who brought them in."

"You got them on my time, using my name, my money, my agency, and my creativity." I tried to keep my voice under control.

"Well, that's debatable. I'm a partner, so it's my time, and you're discounting Ralph and Cory's creativity. But it doesn't matter. The clients decide where they go, and they chose to follow me. You abandoned them. I picked up the pieces. How can you fault them for that?"

"I don't fault them, I fault you. You said that you would cover for me."

"I did exactly what I said I would. I took care of the clients."

"No matter how you spin this, you're a weasel, Kyle. I trusted you, and you stabbed me in the back while I was taking care of my wife. There are special places in hell for people like you."

"Don't get all moral on me, pal. This is just business. I'm moving on, and so are my clients."

"I'm taking you down, Kyle. And that traitor Ralph. You're not getting away with this."

For a moment he was speechless. Then he said, "Well, good luck with that." He hung up.

McKale had been right about him all along.

I struggled over whether or not I should tell McKale and decided to keep it from her until I knew how bad things were. As usual she could tell something was wrong. "Did you ever get hold of Kyle?"

"Yes." I sat down in the chair next to her hospital bed.

"What's going on?" Helpless and vulnerable, she gazed at me.

"You know, usual problems. Bottlenecks and deadlines. I need to go back to work Monday." I reached for her hand and squeezed it.

She looked at me sadly. "I know you do. I'm sorry I've taken so much of you."

"You haven't taken anything that wasn't yours," I said.

A faint smile played on her lips. "So how's Kyle doing?"

"He's been busy," I said, trying to hide my anger.

"I bet. I really misjudged him." She rolled her eyes as if she couldn't believe her own stupidity.

I looked at her for a moment, then said, "Yeah. He's been . . . unbelievable."

"We should give him a really big Christmas bonus this year."

I couldn't stand it anymore. "I've got to use the bathroom," I said. I walked down the hall to the bathroom, locked myself inside, then kicked the plastic garbage can until it broke.

CHAPTER

Eleven

McKale came home today. As joyful as her homecoming is to me, I now fully face the reality that our life will never be the same. It could be worse. I could have come home alone.

Alan Christoffersen's diary

Even with my world in shambles, the day McKale came home was like Christmas. At least until I put her to bed. Then reality set in. There were about a hundred phone messages. Some were calls of condolence, but the majority of them were collection calls. I sat with a pen and paper and wrote them all down.

The collection calls came more than once, growing steadily more intense and threatening.

It wasn't just McKale who was bad with money. Even though my father was an accountant, I never inherited his fiscal discipline. Madgic had taken off like a bottle rocket, and McKale and I wanted everything right away. We purchased the largest home we could get approved for, expensive cars, vacations, and pretty much everything else we wanted. We ate out almost every night. McKale wasn't much of a cook. She was fond of saying, "The only thing I can make are reservations."

On top of that, McKale was generous to a fault and gave to about every charity that came along—from the March of Dimes to the Save a Greyhound Society. We had boxes of unopened Girl Scout cookies in our pantry. Whenever we realized we'd run out of money, I'd get upset for a while, then McKale would say, "You're smart. You'll make more."

Even before the accident (and the demise of the agency), we were in trouble. We were late on all of our bills, had a second mortgage on our home, and our credit cards were maxed out. Financially, we had been walking a tightrope. And someone had just cut one end of our rope.

McKale was responsible for paying the bills, and, obviously, she hadn't done it in a while. In addition to the phone messages, there was a large pile of bills on the ground near the back door. The first time I started through it, I lost my resolve and walked away.

Someone once said, "We can deny reality, but we can't deny the consequences of denying reality." The first of the consequences manifested on Sunday afternoon. As I was cleaning up after lunch, the doorbell rang. I opened to two men. The man in front was about my size and build, though balding and a decade or so older. The second man was sandy haired and looked like a linebacker for the Seattle Seahawks. The first man did the talking.

"Are you Alan Christoffersen?"

"Yes."

"We're from Avait Leasing. We're here to repossess a Lexus Sports Coupe and a Cadillac Escalade."

My eyes darted back and forth between the two. "Look, my wife just got out of the hospital. Is there something we can work out?"

"Sorry, we're way past that. If you would show us to the cars."

I looked at him for any sign of mercy, but there was none. He was there to do his job. "They're in the garage. I'll open it." The men stepped aside as I walked out the front door. I opened the garage by the keypad. "Give me a minute to get our things out of the cars."

"No problem."

I collected our belongings—sunglasses, CDs, cell phone chargers—the usual stuff. When I was done, I removed the car keys from the key rings, then handed them to the man. He threw the Escalade key to his associate then climbed into my Lexus. "Sorry."

I watched them drive away in our cars. I shut the garage door and went back inside.

"Who was at the door?" McKale asked.

I frowned. "Leasing company. They just repossessed our cars."

"Sorry." She looked away from me.

"Don't worry about it," I said. "They're just cars." The truth is, I felt like a lowlife.

Things just got worse. That night as I sorted through mail, I came across the first of the medical bills. More than a quarter million dollars. *I can handle this*, I told myself. *Just don't panic. Don't panic. McKale needs you.*

I panicked.

CHAPTER

Twelve

Something remarkable happened today.
McKale's leg began to move. We're not
breaking out the champagne yet, but
could it be that our luck has finally
changed?

Alan Christoffersen's diary

Monday morning, I got McKale up at six. I bathed, toileted, and dressed her. I got her into her chair, then made her breakfast. As I went about this routine, I thought of that saying, *Today is the first day of the rest of your life*. It fit, just not as optimistically as it was intended. This was my new daily routine—something I would do until the two of us were old and gray.

I hated to leave her alone, but I had no choice. It would have to happen someday. "You sure you'll be all right today?"

"Yes. We need to get used to this," she said.

I kissed her on the forehead, then went to get myself ready. While I was showering, McKale screamed, "Al! Come here, quick!"

I pulled a towel around myself and rushed dripping wet into the room. McKale was smiling. It was the first time I had seen her smile since the accident.

"What?"

"Look," she said. To my amazement one of McKale's legs was moving. "Something's happening."

"Do you have feeling in it?"

"No. But it feels like it wants to move."

My heart leapt. It was the first hope I'd felt in weeks. "Whatever you're doing," I said, "just keep doing it."

"I'm not doing anything," she said. "It just started moving on its own."

Finally, I thought, *something good has happened. Thank you, God.*

CHAPTER

Thirteen

Today I went back to the office for the first time since I ran out. It was like returning to the aftermath of a house fire—walking through steaming ruins and charred remains. Falene was the lone survivor of the inferno.

Alan Christoffersen's diary

Fortunately our bad credit hadn't entirely caught up to us before I had leased a handicap van. I had gone from a luxury sports car to a handicap van. It was a fitting symbol of our new reality.

I arrived at the office at ten minutes to nine. The place looked as if it had been deserted during a lunch break. The lights and computers were still on. Pens and papers were still at desks. It was like one of those episodes of *Unsolved Mysteries*. Unfortunately this was no mystery. It was Kyle. More than half the awards were gone, leaving bare hooks on the conference room wall. In my office, someone had gone through my file cabinet, and there were file folders scattered around my desk. My Rolodex was missing.

I was still in my office when Falene opened the front door. I walked out to meet her. She smiled wryly when she saw me. "Welcome back," she said. We embraced. "I tried to tell you."

"I know." I looked around the office. "Looks like the Grinch struck early."

"He even took the last can of Who-Hash." She shook her head. "Speaking of Grinch, did you ever talk to creepy Kyle?"

"Yes."

"What did he say?"

"Basically, he said he left because I had abandoned the agency. He only had the clients' best interests at heart."

"Wow, what a hero," she said snidely. "Typical Kyle spin. The only interest Kyle has ever had is his own. You know, he started this before McKale was hurt."

I looked at her in surprise. "What?"

"The day before you pitched Wathen, he told me what he was doing and asked if I would go with him. I was going to tell you after the Wathen pitch. But then everything went crazy."

This revelation put everything into perspective. "That freaking weasel," I said. I looked down at my desk and wondered if Kyle himself had ransacked it.

"A weasel he is," Falene said. She rested her hands on her hips. "So where do we begin, boss?"

"I want you to call our client list and set up meetings with anyone who will meet with me."

"Do I have permission to use guilt?"

"Absolutely. Do we have any new leads?"

"There have been a few inquiries. No one big, but they can help keep the lights on. I have them written down in my office. I was keeping them from Kyle."

"Good girl."

We walked off to our separate offices. I spent the morning following up leads and talking to Steve, our accountant. Financially, things weren't quite as grim as it had seemed, not good, but not totally catastrophic either. At least not yet. Several large receivables had come in, and we had about twelve thousand dollars in the bank—

enough to cover our payables. Around two o'clock, Falene came into my office.

"I'm headed down for a salad. Want something?"

"Thanks, but I need to go home and check on McKale. How are the calls going?"

"Okay. Wathen says he's very sorry, but they're just too far along to change course. But he'll keep us in mind for future projects."

I shook my head. "It's only been four weeks."

"I know. He sounded kind of dodgey. I'm sure Kyle's been working him over. But Coiffeur, iTex, and DynaTech are willing to meet next week."

"It's a start. Good job, Falene."

"Thanks. And how is McKale?"

I smiled. "Her leg was moving this morning."

"That's wonderful, isn't it?"

"It makes everything else seem manageable." I stood and began gathering a few files to take with me.

"Will you be coming back today?"

"Tomorrow," I said.

"I'll see you tomorrow then. And don't worry, Al. We'll make it. We'll make Madgic bigger than it was before."

I looked up and smiled at her. "By the way, I'm promoting you to Vice President."

A broad smile crossed her face. "Thank you." She hugged me. "See? Things are looking up already."

CHAPTER

Fourteen

This evening I rushed McKale back to the hospital. More trouble. I feel as if the jaws of Hell have gaped after us. Where is God?

McKale was sitting in her wheelchair in the den when I got home. She had a book in her lap, but she wasn't reading. She was just staring ahead at the wall. "Hey, girl," I said. "I'm home."

She slowly turned to look at me. Her leg was still moving, but her smile was gone. "I wish the fall had killed me."

"McKale . . ."

Her eyes watered. "This is my new life, pushing around the house, chained to this chair."

I put my arms around her. "Give it some time."

She looked down. "I'm sorry, I don't feel well," she said softly. "I think I have a fever."

I kissed her forehead then felt it with my cheek. Her skin was moist and very hot. "You're burning. Why didn't you call me?"

"You have so much work. I didn't want to bother you."

"Come on, Mickey, you know better than that. I better check your temperature. Where do we keep the thermometer?"

"It's downstairs in the guest room medicine cabinet."

I retrieved the thermometer and held it under her tongue. She was running a temperature of 104°. "You're hot. I better call the doctor," I said.

I couldn't get hold of Dr. Hardman, but the doctor

on call told me to bring her in. Forty-five minutes later, I checked McKale back into the Overland emergency room. The staff checked her vitals, blood pressure, and temperature, then took blood and urine samples. Her fever had risen to 105°.

Within a half hour, Dr. Probst, a compact red-head in his late fifties, had her moved from the ER to the ICU where they put tubes back into her arms and a PIC line directly into her jugular vein, to fill her with antibiotics. The staff moved in a quiet, urgent manner, and the more I watched, the more concerned I became. I stayed by McKale's side the whole time, holding her hand. She said very little through it all, though she moaned occasionally. When the motion had settled a little, the doctor asked to speak to me outside the room.

"You're her partner?" he asked.

"I'm her husband. What's happening?"

"It appears your wife has developed a urinary tract infection from her catheter. Unfortunately it's gotten into her bloodstream, and she's septic." He looked at me as if waiting for the gravity of his words to settle.

"What does that mean? You give her more antibiotics?"

He looked at me solemnly. "This is extremely serious. We could lose her."

"Lose her? It's just an infection."

"Infections are never that simple, especially when the body has already been weakened. When they reach this stage, they're very dangerous."

"So what do you do?"

"We've upped her antibiotics. She's on a pretty powerful dosage. Now we carefully monitor her and wait to see how her body responds. We've also sedated her. A fever this high can be quite uncomfortable."

I raked my hair back with my hand. "I can't believe this. This morning we were celebrating. Her leg was moving. We thought she was gaining her nerves back."

"Involuntary muscle spasms," he said. "It's caused by the infection." He had a strained, worried look in his eyes that made me wonder if he was holding back. "I just want you to be prepared." He touched my shoulder then turned and walked away. I watched him go, then I walked down to the men's room. It was a one-occupant bathroom, and I locked the door, then knelt on the tile floor and began to pray.

"God, if you're there, I'll give you anything. Just spare her life. I beg you, don't take her from me." I was on my knees for another ten minutes, until someone tried the door.

How much more humble can you be, I thought. *Kneeling on the floor of a public bathroom. Surely God would hear my prayer.* But the truth is, I felt like I was praying to nothing. I might as well have been praying to the urinal. I got up and went back in to McKale's room. She looked paler already.

"What did he say?" she asked softly.

I didn't want to frighten her. "He said it's just a little infection."

"It doesn't feel so little . . . ," she said, grimacing. She looked up at me. "You must be so tired of all this."

I took her hand. "I'm tired of you going through all this."

"It won't be much longer," she said.

I looked at her quizzically. "What do you mean?"

She closed her eyes. "Stay close to me."

CHAPTER

Fifteen

Don't deceive yourself. Things can always get worse.

Alan Christoffersen's diary

The painkillers did their job, and McKale slept for three more hours. Her temperature had fallen back down to 104° but no lower. Everything else seemed to stay the same, which I suppose was a mixed blessing.

It was around nine or so when she opened her eyes. They were heavy with fever. She tried to speak, but her words were labored and slurred, and, at first, I couldn't understand her. I put my ear next to her mouth. "What did you say?"

Her voice was barely a whisper. "Orcas Island."

I looked at her quizzically. "What?"

"That's where I was going to take you."

Orcas Island is the largest of the San Juan islands, located off the northern coast of Washington. We had celebrated my college graduation there, staying in a bed and breakfast built from a restored farm house. It was one of my fondest memories. I had never been more happy or felt more in love.

"Do you know when I knew I would marry you?"

"When?"

"That day in the tree house. You said you'd never leave me." Her brow furrowed, likely as much from pain as concentration. "Do you remember?"

"Yes."

She swallowed. "You never did."

"And I never will."

After a moment she said, "I'm leaving you." I looked into her face. Her eyes were brimming with tears.

"Don't talk that way, McKale."

"Promise me . . ."

"Don't, Mickey . . ."

"Please. Promise me two things."

My heart was racing. "What?"

"Don't leave me."

"I'll never leave you. You know that."

She swallowed. "I don't want to die alone."

Her words sent a chill through me. "Mickey, don't say that. You're not going to die."

"I'm sorry."

"You're going to beat this. We're going to beat this."

"Okay. Okay." Her words sounded more like pants. She closed her eyes again. A few minutes later a nurse came in. She checked the monitors and frowned.

"What's going on?" I asked.

"Her blood pressure's falling."

"What does that mean?"

She hesitated. "I'm getting the doctor." She walked out of the room.

A minute later, McKale opened her eyes, but she didn't look at me, and she didn't speak.

"You can't leave me, Mick. I can't live without you." She silently looked into my eyes. "If only I had stayed home like you wanted, we wouldn't be here."

She gripped my hand the best she could.

A tear fell down my cheek, and I furtively wiped it away. I looked into her face. "Mickey. What was the other thing?"

She didn't respond.

"You said you wanted me to promise you two things. What's the other thing?"

She looked down for a moment, swallowed, then pursed her lips together, slowly moving them. I put my ear next to her mouth. "What, honey?"

The word seemed like an expulsion. "Live."

I pulled back and looked into her eyes, then she closed hers. The nurse walked back in with the doctor. "You'll need to step back, please," the doctor said.

The doctor gave McKale an injection through her I.V., then took the ventilator tube and carefully inserted it through McKale's mouth and down her throat. My mind was swimming. Things were happening that shouldn't be happening. Her body was shutting down. I don't remember the exact sequence of events. It came at me like a dream where time moved one frame at a time, and disjointed, disembodied phrases hung in the air.

"She's in shock."

"Still dropping."

"Heart rate is dropping."

The motion in the room continued in a growing climax, a swirling, frenzied dance of activity. Then McKale started to breathe differently. She was taking long, strained gasps of air with long pauses between breaths.

"Respiratory failure."

Then came the most frightening sound of all. A single, loud beeping noise joined the cacophony.

"She's going into cardiac arrest."

The doctor frantically began performing CPR. After a minute, he shouted, "Shut off that thing." The beeping stopped. He kept pressing on her chest.

Seven minutes later the dance stopped. My best friend passed away at 12:48 A.M. The last thing I said to her was, "I love you, Mickey. I always will."

CHAPTER

Sixteen

All is lost.

Alan Christoffersen's diary

A social worker came in and stood next to me. I don't know how long she was there. I didn't see her enter. She didn't speak at first. She just stood there. Without looking up, I said, "She's gone."

CHAPTER

Seventeen

I would give anything to have her back.
Anything. But I have nothing to barter
with. Not even my life. Especially my life.
What could a life as wretched as mine be
worth?

The next two days passed in a foggy parade of events. The people at the mortuary pretty much dragged me through it all—an unwilling participant in an unwanted production. I remembered the mechanical nature in which my father had acted in the aftermath of my mother's passing. My condemnation was gone. Now it was me mechanically attending to the minutiae of death: I picked out a casket, a headstone, wrote McKale's obituary, signed papers, and selected the dress she was to be buried in—a beaded, black chiffon overlay gown that gathered in front. She had worn the dress at last January's WAF award ceremonies. I thought she was the most beautiful woman in the room.

It became very clear to me just how completely I had shut everyone else out of my life. Outside of each other, McKale and I had no real friends, and the only people we socialized with were on our payroll. I never thought I needed anyone else. I was wrong.

Sam arrived Thursday afternoon with McKale's stepmother, Gloria. I met them at the mortuary. Sam broke down when he saw her. "My little girl," he sobbed. "My little girl."

My father arrived two days later, the day before the funeral. In his typical manner, he said very little, which, frankly, I was glad for. I could see that he hurt for me, and that was enough. He stayed with me and slept in the downstairs guest room.

✦

It rained all that night, and I sat in the kitchen and listened to a million drops pelt the earth. There was no way I could sleep. My father came upstairs to the kitchen at three in the morning. I was sitting at the kitchen table, a cold cup of decaf in front of me, staring at nothing.

"I couldn't sleep either," he said. "Mind if I join you?"

I shook my head.

He pulled out a chair across from me. For a moment, we both sat in silence. Then he cleared his throat. "When your mother died, I felt as if half my body had been amputated. The half with the heart. At first I wasn't sure if I could keep going on. Frankly, I wasn't sure why I would want to." He looked at me softly. "I don't know what I would have done if I didn't have you. I didn't have the luxury of collapse."

"McKale wanted to have children," I said. "But I kept telling her we needed to wait." I rubbed my eyes. "The assumption of tomorrow."

My father had no response, and my words trailed off in silence.

"Do you want to come back home for a while?"

I shook my head. "No."

"How's your business doing?"

"Not well."

"Maybe you should throw yourself into that for a while."

I said nothing. We both sat in silence.

"Dad."

"Yes?"

"How'd you do it?"

"I have no idea." It was some time before he looked at me. "I love you, son."

"I know."

A few minutes later, he went back to his room. I put my head down on the table and cried.

CHAPTER

Eighteen

My heart was buried with her. I would have been satisfied if the rest of me had been buried with her as well. As much as I have thought on this matter, I see no way around the hurt. The only way to remove pain from death is to remove love from life.

Alan Christoffersen's diary

The next morning it was still raining. I showered, shaved, and dressed on autopilot. As I looked at myself in the mirror, I said, *"God hates you."* It was the only explanation for my life. I had loved two women, and He took both of them from me. God hated me. The feelings were mutual.

At 10:45, my father and I drove together to the funeral home. There was an hour-long viewing prior to the funeral. I stood next to the open casket, next to the still body of the woman I loved. Déjà vu. When they shut the lid, I wanted to scream out in anguish. I wanted to climb in with her.

The service was simple. "Nice," I heard someone say. *Nice.* That's like describing a plane crash as *well executed.* The meeting was conducted by an employee from the mortuary, and a pastor, also hired by the mortuary, shared a few words. I don't remember what he said. My mind was a fog. Something about the eternal nature of man. McKale's stepmother, Gloria, a former opera singer, sang a hymn. "How Great Thou Art." Then McKale's father said a few words, or at least tried to. He mostly just wept through his eulogy. There was a prayer, and then the man from the mortuary got up again and gave directions for the burial proceedings.

McKale's father and four of his friends were pallbearers, along with my father. They carried the casket out to the waiting hearse, loaded it in back, then walked to their cars. We drove in a procession less than a half mile, where the pallbearers again took up the casket, carrying it to the top of a small knoll.

After the pallbearers set down the casket, they unpinned their boutonnieres and set them atop the lid. Sam walked up to me. "I carried her when she was a little girl. No father should ever have to endure this."

McKale's grave was near the center of the Sunset Hills cemetery, surrounded by much older graves. The mortuary had set up a canvas canopy that shielded the family from the rain while everyone else huddled beneath umbrellas. The rain never ceased. It was a steady fall that turned into a downpour that, at the conclusion of the burial, sent everyone scampering for their cars.

As the congregation was dispersing, an older woman slowly approached me. I was certain I had never met her, though something about her looked strangely familiar. She was distraught. Her eyes were red and puffy, and her face was streaked with tears. When she was near, she said, "I'm Pamela."

I looked at her without comprehension. "I'm sorry. Do I know you?"

"I'm McKale's mother."

I blinked in confusion. "McKale doesn't have a . . ." Suddenly I understood. I had always thought of her mother as deceased. Seeing her reminded me of every pain-filled moment McKale had felt since the day I met her. The fact that she was here, now, filled me with rage. With all the emotion I held inside, it was all I could do not to explode. "What do you want?"

"I kept telling myself that someday I'd explain everything to her. That day just never came."

"The assumption of tomorrow," I said darkly.

"Excuse me?"

I rubbed my nose. "Do you have any idea how much you hurt her?"

I could see how deeply my words cut her. "I'm sorry."

For a moment, I just looked at her tired, wrinkled face. "You missed out on someone very special. McKale was a beautiful woman. As sorry as I am for my loss, I'm more sorry for yours."

Her eyes welled up with tears. She turned and walked away.

A few minutes later, Sam walked up to me. "You met Pamela." I nodded. He put his arms around me, burying his head on my shoulder. "Do you know how much McKale loved you? You were her world."

"She was mine," I replied. We both cried.

"Keep in touch," he said. Gloria took his arm. "If there's anything you need, Alan."

"Thank you."

They walked, arm in arm, down the slope to their car.

My father walked up to me. He was holding an umbrella. "Are you ready, son?"

I shook my head. "I can't leave her."

He nodded in understanding. "I'll get a ride back with Tex." He offered me his umbrella, but I just shook my head. He put one hand on my shoulder, then he slowly walked off.

I watched him cautiously pick his way down the hill. He had aged a lot in the last few years. I had always had issues with my father. I know, who doesn't? It would seem that blaming our parents for our problems is a favorite national pastime. But at that moment, I felt nothing but sympathy. He had done this, too. And somehow he had endured. He was a better man than I.

As everyone departed, I stood alone next to her grave, the rain bathing me, drenching me completely. I didn't care. I had no place else I wanted to be. A half hour later, only one other person remained. Falene walked up to me. "C'mon, Alan."

I didn't move.

She touched my arm. "C'mon, honey. You're all wet. You'll get sick."

I turned and looked at her, my face more drenched by tears than rain. At that moment the emotional dam broke. "I can't leave her . . ."

Falene wrapped her arms around me and pulled me into

her. She held me, in the rain. She just said over and over, "I'm so sorry. I'm so sorry."

I don't know how long we were there. An eternity. But when I could cry no more, I looked down into her eyes. She, too, was crying. "Come back with me, please." She took my hand. "I'll take care of you."

She led me to her car, then opened the passenger door, and I got in. She climbed in the other side, reached over me, and pulled my seatbelt across my chest. She drove me to her apartment. Neither of us spoke on the way.

CHAPTER

Nineteen

It is in the dark times that the light of
friendship shines brightest.

Alan Christoffersen's diary

When we arrived at her apartment complex, Falene pulled in under a carport, then walked around her car, and opened my door. Her building was four stories high, and her apartment was on the ground level, a half flight down. She unlocked the door and pushed it open. "Go on in," she said.

The small apartment was dark, the blinds half drawn with only a little light coming through their openings. The room smelled like coffee grounds.

Falene helped me off with my coat, laid it over the back of a chair, then took off her own. She turned on a light, then took my hand and led me over to her couch, a small curved sofa with velvet upholstery. "I'll get you some hot tea. Is it warm enough in here for you?"

I nodded even though I hadn't even thought about it. I wasn't sure why I was there or why she had brought me to her home. My experience with models was that they were remarkably self-absorbed. Falene was different. At the agency, Falene had always taken care of me, but I assumed it was because she got paid for it. It had never occurred to me that she really was nurturing.

Falene went back into her bedroom, then came back out when the teakettle began to scream. She had changed into jeans and a sweater. She handed me a towel, then she took the kettle from the heat and poured my cup.

"I hope you like herbal tea. This is orange peppermint. I think it will help soothe you. Would you like sugar?"

I nodded.

She put in a teaspoonful and stirred it. She brought me the cup then sat down next to me. For a moment neither of us spoke. Then I said, "You're the only friend I have."

She frowned. "No. You have a lot of friends."

"No, I don't. Just McKale. She was all I wanted." I took a sip of the tea then set the cup down. "Why have you been so good to me?"

She smiled sadly. "Because you are a wonderful man." She looked down. "I know you don't know very much about me. But when I came to work at Madgic, I didn't really think I was going to stay for long. Kyle talked me into coming, that's what Kyle does, he talks people into things, but I didn't feel like I belonged. And I didn't trust him. I trusted you almost immediately. You made me feel important. At the time I was in a dead-end relationship."

"Carl," I said.

She flinched at his name. "He just used me. And the thing is, some part of me was okay with that. I just thought that was how all men treated women." She looked at me with a pained expression. "Then I met you. No matter how busy you were, you would always take McKale's calls. And even when you were stressed, or something bad had happened, you were always so gentle with her. When she came down to the agency, you treated her like a queen.

At first I didn't believe it could be real. I had never seen a man treat a woman like that, unless he wanted something from her. You were so good to her. You showed me what real love is.

"Do you remember that conversation we had when we were getting ready for the Denver convention?"

"Which one?" I asked.

"You said, 'You can tell a lot about a man by watching how he treats those he doesn't have to be nice to.' I knew you didn't just make that up. I remember that time after the Coiffeur shoot when that waitress knocked a Coke over on you. Carl would have screamed at her until she cried. You weren't happy about it, but you still treated her with respect. I realized I had been settling for mud when there are diamonds out there. You're the reason I dumped Carl, and it's the best thing I've ever done. You saved me from myself."

I didn't say anything. She took my hand.

"McKale once told me that you were the air she breathed. I thought that was the sweetest thing I had ever heard." She looked at me, then said, "Come here." I lay my head on her shoulder, and she wrapped her arms around me. "I'm so sorry, my friend. I wish I could take away your hurt." She held me until I stopped crying. Then she put a pillow down. "Just rest for a moment."

It was the last thing I remembered Falene saying before I fell asleep.

It was a little after eight when I woke the next morning. I had fallen asleep on the couch, and Falene had taken off my shoes and laid a wool blanket over me. There was a scrawled note on the coffee table.

Alan, I had to go on a photo shoot. I had a friend take me over to the cemetery to get your van. It's parked downstairs. Your keys are on the table. I'll be back around two. Make yourself at home. There's coffee in the pot and some Pop-Tarts. (I know you like those.) If you need to go, I understand. Please, please, please call me. I care about you.

Love,
Falene

I put my shoes on then lifted my keys from the table. I wrote "Thank you" over her note. Then I drove home.

CHAPTER

Twenty

There is a moment in all acts when there is no turning back: the step over the cliff, the finger committing to the trigger and the hammer falling, the bullet erupting from the chamber, unstoppable . . .

Alan Christoffersen's diary

Returning to an empty house was harder than I thought it would be. Could be. It seemed the pain increased as I got closer. Two blocks from the house, I almost hyperventilated. I got mad at myself. "Pull yourself together, man."

My father had already gone home. He left a note for me on the kitchen table. It just read: "Eight o'clock flight. Call when you can."

I walked through the house, not sure what I was supposed to do. Not that there weren't things to do. The house was a disaster. There were dishes in the sink, overflowing clothes hampers, fast-food sacks and wrappers on the counters. There were still piles of unopened mail and newspapers inside the door.

At first I lay down, but I couldn't find relief, so I set to washing clothes. As I lifted one of McKale's undershirts, I held it against my face. I could still smell her.

That afternoon the postman came to my door. He held a clipboard and a registered letter.

"You need to sign for this," he said.

"What is it?"

"Registered mail. I just need your signature saying you

received it. Right here." He pointed to a short line. I signed so he'd leave. I shut the door, then opened the envelope. It was a notice from the bank informing me that my house has been foreclosed on and would go up for auction next Thursday. I dropped the letter on the ground. I honestly didn't care. I didn't care about anything. The world had already caved in on me; what did it matter if another brick or two fell?

I didn't eat that night. The idea of putting food in my mouth made me want to gag. Falene called around eight, but I couldn't answer the phone. Not even for her. Grief had settled around me like smog. By nightfall, my heart had become a boxing match, and there were two men inside of me contending for the possession of my future.

Fighting out of the blue corner, in white trunks, is LIFE. And in the red corner, wearing solid black trunks, is DEATH.

The fight had begun even before I was aware of it. Probably the moment I first saw McKale in her hospital bed.

After nine rounds, DEATH has gained the upper hand, showing LIFE no mercy. Constant jabs have left LIFE reeling. LIFE's no longer the cocky prize-belt winner who weeks before paraded around as champ. LIFE has lost his legs. He's on the ropes. DEATH senses victory and moves in for the kill. He's relentless, landing one punch after another. It's painful to watch, folks. LIFE is taking a beating, too tired and dazed to even block the blows.

The crowd senses blood and roars. They don't care who wins, they just want a good fight.

At 2:00 A.M. the battle was in its final rounds. I was sitting at the kitchen table, holding two open bottles of McKale's unused prescriptions—oxycodone and codeine—enough of each to end the fight. On the table in front of me was something to wash them down—an open bottle of Jack Daniel's.

Ironically, in the early months of my advertising agency, I had done some pro-bono work for the Suicide Prevention Association of Seattle. The words I wrote for their radio commercial still resonated with me:

Suicide—a permanent solution to a temporary problem.

A catchy slogan, but the words rang hollow to me. There was nothing temporary about McKale's death. I had lost everything. My business, my cars, my home, and, most of all, my love. There was nothing left—no reason to live except the natural human aversion to death. But even that was waning. I could feel it being pushed out by overwhelming pain, despair, and anger. Anger at life. Anger at God. Most of all anger at myself.

I looked at the pills. What was I waiting for? It was time to get on with it. Time to get this show on the road. I poured the pills into my hand.

I was about to cross the point of no return, when something happened. Something unlike anything I'd experienced before. Something I believe came from God—or part of His world.

When I was a child, my mother taught me about God. My mother was a big fan—even as she was dying. *Especially* as she was dying. She would pray, not as some do, repeating a script or chant, or shouting out to an empty universe, but as if He were actually in the same room. There were times, during her prayers, that I opened my eyes and looked around to see who she was talking to.

At that very moment, a fraction before I crossed *the line*, someone spoke to me. I don't know if the words were audible, as they seemed to come both from and to my mind, but they came with an authority far greater than my own mind could muster. Just six words. Six words that stopped me cold.

Life is not yours to take.

My first reaction was to look around to see who had spoken. When I realized I was truly alone, I dropped the pills on the ground. Then another voice came to me. A softer voice. The voice of my love.

"Live."

For the first time, I fully understood the promise McKale had asked me to make. She knew me. She knew I wouldn't want to live without her.

I fell to my knees and began to cry. I don't remember what happened after that. I don't remember a thing.

CHAPTER

Twenty-one

They have not taken my home, just the brick and mortar that once housed it.

Alan Christoffersen's diary

I woke the next morning to the sound of someone opening my door. The house was dark. Even though the sun had risen, the skies were a gray ceiling, typical for this time of year. At least it was no longer raining.

The door opened before I could get up. A man, well-dressed in a gray wool suit with a white shirt and a crimson tie, walked into my foyer, followed by two older women. They flipped on the lights.

It was one of the women who saw me first. "Oh, my."

The other two turned and looked at me as I stumbled to my feet. There I was, disheveled and unshaven, a bottle of booze on the table and pills scattered on the floor. The women looked at me fearfully.

"Excuse me," the man said, sounding more annoyed than sorry, "we were told the home was vacant."

"It's not," I said.

"Clearly." The man reached into his coat pocket and pulled out a business card. He stepped toward me, offering his card. "I'm Gordon McBride, from Pacific Bank. You are aware that the home has been foreclosed on."

I didn't take the card. "You don't waste much time, do you?"

He looked uncomfortable. "You know what they say, 'Time is money.'"

"It's not."

"We can come back later," one of the women said.

"No, it's all right," I said. "Help yourself. I'm still getting my things. The house is a mess."

They walked into the living room. I bent down and scooped the pills back into their bottles, then went to my bedroom as they toured the rest of the house. I showered and dressed. Before they left, Mr. McBride found me. "When are you moving out?"

I felt like a squatter in my own home. Technically I guess I was. "Soon," I replied. "Real soon."

I meant what I said about leaving. I couldn't wait to get out. Without McKale, this was no longer my home. I felt no more connected to this place than the public library. Now that it had officially been claimed by others, it was time for me to go. The only question was *where?*

CHAPTER

Twenty-two

I believe that in spite of the chains we bind ourselves with, there's a primordial section of the human psyche that still yearns to roam free.

Alan Christoffersen's diary

The first spark of the idea came to me as I watched the banker back his silver Audi out of my driveway. At that moment, one of my elderly neighbors walked by—Mr. Jorgensen from three houses down. Mr. Jorgensen was wearing a polyester baby-blue jacket and straw hat and was leaning against a cane. He had Parkinson's and was shaking as he walked. I don't know why seeing him triggered what it did—who knows where ideas come from? But at that moment it was clear to me what I had to do. Perhaps the only thing left for me to do. I needed to walk far away.

In retrospect that moment wasn't really the first time the thought of walking long distance had crossed my mind. When I was fifteen I read a book about a guy who walked across America, and ever since then I had secretly wanted to follow in his steps. Literally.

I don't think I'm alone in this fantasy. I believe that in spite of the chains we bind ourselves with, there's a primordial section of the human psyche that is still nomadic and still yearns to roam free. We see evidence of this in the walkabouts of the Australian aborigines and the Spirit Walk of the native Americans. We also see it cautiously peeking out its head in our own culture, surfacing in our literature and music. From Thoreau to Steinbeck to

Kerouac—each generation believes they have discovered the dream anew.

But it's not new. Every generation has dreamed of roaming. Deep in our hearts everyone wants to walk free.

Maybe not *everybody*. When I told McKale about my secret desire she said, "Not me. I'd rather fly."

"But then you'd miss everything," I said.

"Not *every*thing. Just the boring stuff."

"No, the *real* stuff. The real America. The little towns with names like Chicken Gristle and Beaverdale."

"Right," she said. "The boring stuff."

I pressed on. "You mean to tell me that you really have never wanted to just pack up and start walking?"

"Never. But you hang on to that dream, you crazy old coot."

A quote from one of my favorite comedians came to mind: "Anyplace is within walking distance if you have the time."

That's all I had left. Time. Far more of it than I wanted. I retrieved the Rand McNally road atlas from my den, opened it to a map of the continental U.S. and spread it out on the kitchen table. I studied it for a moment, then I went through the kitchen drawers looking for string. The closest thing I could find was a package of shoelaces. I tore the package open and put the plastic tip of one end of a shoelace on the city of Bellevue, then stretched the shoelace to the opposite side of the map, moving it up and down the east coast to determine the furthest point reachable by foot. Key West, Florida. Key West was as far as I could go from where I stood. That was where I was going to walk. An hour later I called Falene.

She was relieved to hear from me. "Are you all right?"

"Yeah. I'm sorry I haven't called."

"It's okay. I've just been so worried."

"I need to ask you a favor."

"Anything."

"This is a big one. I need you to shut everything down. Sell everything at the agency, the furniture, computers, everything. Put it on eBay or Craigslist. I'll text you a bank account number to deposit whatever you bring in from it."

"What about your personal things?"

"I don't care. Keep whatever you want. Throw the rest away."

"What about your awards?"

The *awards*. My golden idols. "Throw them away."

"What?"

"Also, there are the things in my home. The furniture."

"But you need it."

"Not anymore. The bank foreclosed on my house."

Falene groaned.

"There's more than a hundred thousand dollars of furniture and junk in here. I guess put it all on eBay or something."

"My aunt owns a furniture consignment store," Falene said. "They can send a truck over."

"Great. Return the van to the leasing company." I

paused. "And there's Cinnamon . . ." Cinnamon was McKale's horse. "Just see if the livery owner wants her."

"I understand," she said.

"You can keep half of what you bring in, just put the rest into my account."

"Where will you be?"

"I'm going for a walk."

"Where to?"

"Key West."

For a moment she said nothing. I think she was trying to decide whether or not I was joking. "You mean Florida?"

"Yes."

"You're walking to Key West, Florida," she said incredulously. "Why?"

"It's the farthest place I can walk from here."

"You're serious about this," she said sadly. "When are you leaving?"

"This afternoon. As soon as I finish packing."

"I need to see you before you go. I can be there in forty-five minutes. Don't leave before I get there. Promise me."

"I'll wait," I said.

"I'll be right over. Don't leave," she said again and hung up.

I dialed Steve, my accountant. I instructed him to pay off all our bills, then file to dissolve our corporation and close out all our bank accounts, transferring any extra money into my personal account. He was disappointed to lose our business but not all that surprised. With all that had transpired in the last month, anything was possible.

We went over the agency's remaining receivables, then

I gave him Falene's phone number in case he ran into any problems. I thanked him for his service and told him I'd check back with him in a few months. His final words of advice to me were, "Wear sunscreen."

Falene arrived within the hour. I could tell she had been crying. We embraced, then we walked from room to room, talking about the furniture. There was really nothing I couldn't leave behind. We ended up in the foyer.

"So, you'll help me?"

"Yes. But half is too much. I'll just take my salary."

"It's going to be a lot of work. You'll have to hire someone to help you."

"I'll get my brother. He doesn't have a job."

I handed her a piece of paper. "Here's my bank account number. I talked to Steve just a few minutes ago, he's going to close out the corporate accounts and transfer the balance into that account as well. I told him that if he had any questions, he could call you. Is that okay?"

"Of course."

I looked her in the eye. "Are you sure you can do this?"

"Of course. I'm Vice President now, remember?"

I looked at her wryly. "But are you *sure* you want to?"

"I'm *sure* I don't. What I want is for everything to go back to how it was. But that's not an option, is it?"

"If only," I said.

She glanced at the paper, then put it in her purse. "How will I get hold of you?"

"You won't. But I'll call from time to time."

She didn't know what else to say.

"Thank you, Falene. Your friendship is the only good

thing to come out of all this. You are one of the finest people I've ever met."

She put her arms around me, and we held each other for a few moments. As we parted, she wiped tears from her eyes. "I wish you wouldn't do this."

"What else is there?"

She looked at me with a dark, sad expression, then kissed my cheek. "Be safe." She wiped her eyes as she walked out of the house. I wondered if I'd ever see her again.

There were only two things I couldn't discard. First, McKale's jewelry. McKale didn't have a lot of jewelry—she preferred a bare look—but over time, I had bought her some nice things. It all had sentimental value, and each piece reminded me of where we were when I gave it to her and how she'd responded. I took her wedding ring and slipped it over a gold rope-chain and put it around my neck. The rest, an opal ring, a ruby-and-emerald necklace, and a pink sapphire-and-diamond brooch, I put in a small pouch and put it in my pocket.

The other things I valued were my journals. Twenty-plus years' worth. As I looked through them, I came across a dark brown leather journal that I bought on a trip to Italy several years earlier and hadn't written in yet. The leather was soft, more of a wrap than a book cover, with a single leather thong that wrapped around the entire book. I decided that this would make a suitable road diary.

I put the rest of the journals in a box and taped it up with a note to Falene to send the box to my father's house.

McKale would want her clothes to go to a women's shelter, so I put her things in big boxes and marked them for Falene to deliver. With one exception. I took one of her silk camisoles. Then I began packing for my walk.

One of my agency's former clients was a local retailer called Alpinnacle, a vendor of high-end hiking equipment. It was our smallest account. I didn't usually pitch accounts their size, but in their case, I made an exception as McKale and I loved to hike, and we were fans of the company's products.

Every year we produced a catalog for them, and the product samples we brought in for the photo shoot were left with us to distribute amongst our employees. I always got first choice of the booty and had claimed several backpacks, a portable, one-burner propane stove, a poncho, a down sleeping bag with a self-inflating pad, and a one-man tent. I could use all of it. I selected the best of the packs and filled it with the gear.

We kept our camping gear in a closet in the basement, and I went downstairs to collect other things I would need: an LED flashlight/radio with a hand crank, fire starter, and a Swiss Army knife. I put it all in the pack.

While I was rooting through the closet, I came across my favorite hat: an Akubra Coober Pedy, an Australian fur-felt hat with a leather band adorned with a small opal

(Coober Pedy is a famed source of Australian opals). I had purchased the hat six years earlier on a business trip to Melbourne. As much as I liked the hat, I rarely wore it, because McKale mocked me when I did. She said I looked like the guy on *The Man from Snowy River*, which I personally thought was a good thing. It had a wide, sturdy brim and was made for the outback weather, sun, sleet, and rain. I put it on. It still fit comfortably.

I went back upstairs and retrieved my Ray-Ban Wayfarers sunglasses. Also, a roll of toilet paper, six pairs of socks, two pairs of cargo pants, a parka, a canteen, and five pairs of underwear.

I pulled on my pants, heavy wool socks, a T-shirt, and a Seattle SuperSonics sweatshirt. Fortunately, I had good hiking boots. They were lightweight, sturdy, and broken in. I sat down and laced them up. Then I slung the pack over my shoulder. It wasn't too heavy, maybe twenty pounds.

The door locked automatically behind me, and without a single key in my pocket, I stood outside on the front patio. Then, without looking back, I began to walk.

CHAPTER

Twenty-three

I have decided on a destination; the path
is but detail. I have begun my walk.

Alan Christoffersen's diary

Chyan li jr sying, shr yu dzu sya. *The journey of a thousand miles begins with a single step.* I read that in a Chinese fortune cookie. Technically I suppose, it wasn't really a fortune— more of a proverb—and probably wasn't even Chinese. It was likely just some American copywriter churning out yarns for a cookie company. I suppose all those years in advertising had made me cynical.

Whatever its origin, the proverb was applicable. Mentally and emotionally, I found that a walk as far as Key West was a little hard to wrap my mind around. My ultimate destination might as well have been China. I needed an interim target, a destination that was far enough to motivate me but close enough not to break my will. That place was on the other side of the state. I set my mind on Spokane.

The drive from Seattle to Spokane along I-90 is about four hours by car. But I wasn't traveling by car, and 90 is an interstate. The Highway Patrol would definitely have some problems with my route. The preferred (and by "preferred" I mean "legal") route for bikers and hikers is Highway 2, a scenic two-lane road that climbs through the Cascade mountains up to Stevens Pass, one of Washington's ski resorts. I knew that at that time of the year there would be snow at the pass, but I pushed it from my mind. I'd deal with that when I got there.

I followed 132nd Avenue north to Redmond Road, then walked about six miles northeast into Redmond. By the time I arrived at the city center, it was around two in the afternoon, and the traffic was heavy.

I was a bit conspicuous traveling through downtown Redmond with a backpack and sleeping bag slung over my back, and I drew a lot of curious glances, but I didn't care. The first casualty of hitting rock bottom is vanity.

From the heart of Redmond, I continued north up Avondale Road. The walk was flat, and the side of the road was wet and spongy, carpeted with copper-hued pine needles fallen from the trees that lined the route. As I walked farther away from the city, I noticed that my mood softened a little. The sounds of birds and water, the rhythmic fall of my feet, and the cool, fresh air untied my mind from the craziness of the night before. I've always believed that a good walk in the woods is as effective as psychotherapy. Nature is, has always been, the greatest of healers.

By Woodinville—about sixteen miles from Bellevue— my legs already felt tired, which was a bad omen. Even though I was an avid hiker and runner, the last four weeks I had sacrificed everything to be with McKale, including exercise. Not surprisingly, I had lost muscle and gained weight—enough at least that my pants were snug at the waist.

There was a Safeway grocery store at the edge of town, and I stopped in for supplies and to get something to eat.

I bought two quart bottles of water, a pint bottle of orange juice, a box of peanut butter and chocolate energy bars, two boxes of frosted blueberry Pop-Tarts, two Braeburn apples, a Bartlett pear, a bag of trail mix, and a sixteen-ounce bag of jerky.

People instinctively fear people with beards (like Santa Claus, or the homeless guy who sits next to you on the bus), when, historically speaking, it should be mustaches we most worry about (e.g., Hitler, Stalin, John Wilkes Booth).

Alan Christoffersen's diary

After some deliberation, I purchased a travel pack of shampoo and a package of disposable razors and shaving gel. I had considered letting my beard grow until I looked like one of the ZZ Top guys, but decided against it. The truth is, I've never liked wearing beards. I grew a goatee once, but McKale said it hurt to kiss me and threatened to withhold her lips until I shaved it off. (She also told me that it made me look like Satan. I don't know how she knew what Satan looked like, but the goatee came off that night.)

My pack was noticeably heavier as I left the Safeway.

I continued walking north until I reached Highway 522, and turned east. I was finally free of suburbia. The forest around me was overgrown on both sides, thick with ferns, evergreens, and lichen-flocked black cottonwoods.

In spite of the ballast I'd added, the walk became easier as the road gradually descended, and my pack seemed to be pushing me downhill.

Seattle is amphibious. Even when I couldn't see water, I could hear it somewhere, an underground stream or viaduct or a roadside waterfall. Under these conditions other cities would mold or rot—but on this side of Washington, wet is the natural state of things—like a salamander's back.

By four-thirty darkness was already starting to fall. As daylight faded, the temperature dropped to the low forties. I decided not to take chances with my remaining light and find a place to camp.

I had just reached Echo Lake when I encountered a bank rising 30 feet or more into thick forest, providing a screen from the road. I climbed the bank, grabbing on to ferns and foliage to avoid slipping on the muddy hill. At the top, I looked down and saw a small inlet. I wasn't the first to discover the site. There was a flat area where someone had camped before, evidenced by rocks gathered into a fire pit.

I hiked down the ravine to the edge of the water, found a dry spot, and laid down my pack. I looked around again to make sure I was alone, then I pulled the tent out of my pack.

Even though I had written the brochure for this tent, I'd never actually assembled it. Fortunately, it was as easy to construct as I had promised. I was glad for this. Whether I was selling tents or politicians, more times than not, I wrote my pitches based on what the product should be, not necessarily what it was. This made me a professional liar. At least I was right about the tent.

I rolled out my self-inflating pad, then laid out my sleeping bag, a down-filled mummy sack. I took off my clothes, climbed inside, and lay back with my head sticking outside of the tent's vinyl screen door. The sky was veiled behind layers of thin, black clouds. I looked at the fire pit.

When I was twelve years old, in scouting, my scoutmaster told us that the first thing one should do when lost in the wilderness is start a fire. He asked us why, and we offered our answers. *Heat. Warmth. To keep wild animals away. To signal rescuers where we were.*

"All good answers," he said, "but none of them what I'm looking for. You start a fire to keep yourself from panicking."

I should have started a fire. As night descended, so did the panic of my situation. I realized that I was not walking alone. I was being followed by three fellow sojourners: grief, bitterness, and despair. I might get ahead of them for a while, but they always caught up. I wondered what kind of legs they had and how many miles they'd follow me and across how many state lines. The whole way?

I could hardly believe that just that morning I was living in a $2 million home with a computerized home environment system, a king-sized canopy bed with a plush mattress, and Egyptian cotton sheets with a hundred thousand thread count. (I might have exaggerated that last fact.) Now I was living in a tent. My world was upside down. I wanted to tell McKale about it. She'd call me a crazy old coot. She'd say, "I can't believe you're actually doing this." Then she'd say, "Yes I do. You're a dream chaser."

I realized that this was how my life would be from now on—not necessarily living in a tent, but living in contrast to my former existence. Like the Gregorian calendar's *Anno Domini*, my life would likewise be designated, *Before* and *After McKale*.

I had been with her for so long that not only did everything remind me of her, everything I experienced was viewed relative to her—what she liked, hated, laughed at, or endured for my sake.

I couldn't believe I had to live the rest of my life without her.

CHAPTER

Twenty-four

Today I met a man without hands. He is a
living, breathing metaphor of my life.

Alan Christoffersen's diary

Birds woke me. I didn't know what species they were, other than annoying. The racket was probably my fault. They were likely just screeching at me for intruding on their world.

Almost as soon as I woke, the pain returned. If you've known loss, you know what I mean. Every morning since McKale's death had been that way—within moments of consciousness, I felt the heaviness of grief settle over me. If nothing else, grief is, at least, reliable.

I sat up in my tent and rubbed my legs. My calves were sore from the previous day's walk. I figured I had covered close to twenty miles. I hadn't walked that far in one day since McKale signed us up for the Muscular Dystrophy fundwalker. I should have stretched before going to bed. I just didn't think about it. I had too many other things on my mind.

I opened my pack and brought out a Pop-Tart and the bottle of orange juice. There were two Pop-Tarts in a package, but I ate just one and returned the other. I drank the whole bottle of juice. Then I took out my razor and cream and went to the water to shave. The lapping inlet water was cold, and it braced my face as I rinsed off the shaving cream, clouding the water white. *I'm soft,* I thought. *I've become soft.*

McKale's and my idea of roughing it was a hotel without twenty-four-hour room service. I once read that in the Wild West, men would avoid baths because they believed warm water made them weak. They might have been right. Warm water had made me weak.

As I was putting back my razor, my cell phone rang, startling me. I had forgotten that I had it. I instinctively checked to see who was calling, but I didn't recognize the number, so I didn't answer. The phone was my last link to the world I had left behind. It was more than a link— this sleek device was filled with contacts, schedules, and history—a microcosm of the very world I was walking away from. I did what every cell phone user has occasionally fantasized. I hurled the device as far as I could into the lake. It barely made a splash.

I stuffed everything back into my pack, then left my first camp, climbing the tall bank to get back to the road. The hill was slick, and I slipped on the way down the other side, leaving my rear and pack caked with mud and pieces of torn fern. I stood, wiped off my seat and backpack, then started on my walk.

I walked for about two hours before I reached the town of Monroe. I had asked the checker at the Woodinville Safeway about Monroe, and she said the town was nothing. Her assessment was flawed. It was bigger than I expected.

I stopped and stretched at the town's welcome sign. Every town has a sign, like Welcome doormats. While most signs display no more creativity than a name, the more ambitious towns use these signs as advertisements. None of them say what they really mean: OKAY, YOU'RE HERE. SPEND SOME MONEY, THEN GO HOME.

As I walked down Monroe's main street, I was aware that I was being watched from business windows, parking lots, and passing cars. This was a phenomenon that I would never fully get used to but would come to expect. In the smaller towns, a stranger walking through is met with mild suspicion or curiosity and usually both. No doubt at least one of the towns along my route would someday print an article about my appearance that would read like this.

Unidentified, hat-wearing man walks through town

Tuesday afternoon around five p.m., an unidentified man, wearing a hat, walked through town. He left no clues as to why he came and just as quickly departed, leaving some Beauville residents feeling a little dejected. Beauville neighbor Mrs. Wally Earp told the *Bugle*, "I hope he comes back and stays awhile. I think he'd find we can be right hospitable. He didn't even try my apple crisp." Other residents, like Jack Calhoun of 76 Main Street, were glad to see him gone. "A man wearing that kind of hat can't be up to any good. Probably a socialist." Millicent Turnpikes, owner of Millie's Glad Rags on Nutmeg Street, had this to say: "I don't know what he was up to, but it was a fine hat."

The unidentified man and his hat were unavailable for comment.

A half-mile into Monroe, I passed a one-story, stucco building with a raptor dinosaur perched on the sign out front. (I'm not sure what the raptor had to do with braces, though the specimen displayed a fine, nicely aligned row of flesh-tearing ivories.)

DR. BILL'S ORTHODONTICS

Good advertising, I thought. *Every boy in town will want braces.*

I had long exhausted the carbs from my one-Pop-Tart breakfast, but I felt more unsociable than hungry, and the restaurants I encountered all looked crowded, so I just kept on walking. I passed a handful of espresso shacks, which in Washington is a frequent and welcomed phenomenon. I'd wager that Seattle has more coffee shops per capita than anywhere else in the world. No wonder that it's the birthplace of Starbucks.

Near the end of the town was a Jack in the Box drive-through. The restaurant was probably as crowded as any of the diners I'd already passed, but this was my last chance for a hot meal, and my stomach was now growling at me, so I went inside.

As I entered, I noticed the furtive, anxious glances of diners already seated. I had no beard, so I figured there must be something about the backpack that made them nervous. My mind constructed this tongue twister:

Unsettled Seattler unsettles the settled.

Just my ad-guy mind amusing itself. Or gone haywire. I ordered myself an egg and sausage sandwich and two cartons of orange juice, then sat down in a vacant corner to eat. There was a *Seattle Times* on the table next to me, and I grabbed it to look over the headlines. I didn't see the man walk up to me.

"Hey, sorry to bother you man, but could you help me get some breakfast?"

I looked up. My petitioner had a bushy beard and wild hair that looked like it hadn't been washed for a year or more. There were deep scars across his chin, but they were not as noticeable as the brown, wart-like spots that marred his skin as if mud had been splashed on his face. He was wearing light blue hospital scrubs that were loose and fell far enough below his waist to almost expose him. I was wondering why he didn't pull them up when I noticed his hands. He had none. From the look of the stubs, they appeared to have been surgically removed at his wrists. *What would require the amputation of both hands?*

". . . A big meal with pancakes is three dollars," he said.

Just a few days ago this man would have made me uncomfortable. But now I felt none of that. I suppose I felt a kinship of sorts. We were both homeless. I opened my wallet and pulled out four dollars. "Here."

"Thanks." He reached forward, pressing the bills between his two stubs. "I appreciate it."

He walked up to the front, dropped the bills on the counter, and said something to an anxious young woman at the cash register who wouldn't look at him. A few moments later, he returned to the dining room with a sack of food. He sat down at the table next to me. I looked to see how he would eat pancakes without hands.

"Thanks again," he said to me.

"Don't mention it," I said. I returned to the paper but I kept looking up at him. He lifted a pancake with his stubs and began to eat. After a moment I asked, "What's your name?"

He turned and looked at me. "Will."

"Nice to meet you, Will," I said. He extended one arm. It was a little awkward, but I shook it. "What happened to your hands?"

He didn't seem bothered by my question. "The thing is, I like bikes," he said.

"Bikes?"

"Yeah. Mountain bikes. Diamondback. And hills. There's something about hills. It's a seduction, you know. Hills are a seduction. I had an accident on a hill. The doc-

tors, well, they saved my life, but they had to take these."
He held up his arms. "But they saved my life. That's good."

"Is it?" I said.

He looked at me quizzically, then reached down and
lifted the pancake and took another bite. There were little
plastic containers of syrup on his tray, but he clearly had
no way of opening them.

"Do you want me to open your syrup for you?"

"Yeah. Thanks."

I peeled back one end of the lid on the container and
poured syrup over his pancakes. I didn't know why I was
so interested in this man. "Do you have family?" I asked.

He looked away, and I noticed he twitched. "Yes."

"Where do you live?" I asked.

"The shelter when it's cold."

"Like now?"

"This isn't cold."

"Is there a shelter around here?"

"It's in Seattle."

I wondered what he was doing in Monroe. Of course, I
could ask myself the same thing. It had never occurred to
me that the homeless I encountered downtown near my
agency might have plans and schedules. "What do you do
during the day?"

"I walk," he said. "I used to walk around the mall. But
they don't like me there much. Sometimes the security
hassles me. One time they beat me up for fun, so I don't
go so much in person. I just think about it. It's easier to
just pretend to go. It's better to pretend. Or wherever. I
can pretend to go anywhere. To a movie. To a restaurant.

I can go to New York City or Paris or Moscow. None of it don't cost a dime. It's the same, just easier. But it's better to read books."

"You like books?" I asked.

"Yeah. But I don't like the bookstores anymore. They don't like me there. They've never beat me up, but they have food in the bookstores and coffee, except the Crown bookstores, but there's not so many of them anymore. You shouldn't have coffee and food around books. It's not right. I like King."

"Stephen King?"

He leaned forward. "Do you know Mr. King?"

"I know of his books."

"I like Dumas and Mitchum. I don't know about text-books." His expression suddenly turned grave. "In school, the teacher had the teacher book. It had all the answers in it. Why don't they just give the teacher book to the students? Then they'd have all the answers. Isn't that why they go to school?

"You know, everywhere I go, I just . . . I keep looking for the teacher book. If I could just find it, then it could be . . ." He looked me over. I felt like he was trying to decide whether he could trust me or not. He leaned forward and said in a softer voice, "I found it once, you know. I found it and started to read it, then I passed out before I could get all the answers. I was on the ground, unconscious. It was too much to know. Like, in the Bible, when there are things that people just can't know, so God seals them in books. Now I just can't find the teacher book. If I could just find it . . . it has all the answers."

"It doesn't have all the answers," I said. "Nothing has all the answers."

He grimaced. "The teacher book has the answers."

"There is no teacher book," I said angrily.

He looked at me curiously, then he said, "You don't know what can happen in a blink. Time is nothing. The whole history of humanity may just be in a blink. We don't know. I think I sometimes blink and read every book in the world. Every book in the world but the teacher book."

"There is no teacher book," I shouted. "There are no answers. Horrific things happen for no damn reason. Just look at your hands."

He looked at me as if I was crazy. Others in the dining room were looking at me too. After a moment he said, "I don't read books anymore, I pretend them. And I preserve them. Books used to be beautiful, they had this . . . you know . . . board cover. You need to preserve them. Especially with all the coffee and food they have at bookstores now."

I finished eating my sandwich, chugged down my last carton of juice, then stood. I didn't want to talk to him anymore. I pulled a five-dollar bill out of my wallet and dropped it on the table next to his pancakes. "That's for lunch."

"Thanks." He went back to his breakfast.

I lifted my pack over my shoulder and started walking again. About a block from the Jack in the Box was the turnoff to Highway 2. Even though I'd already traveled nearly 25 miles, I felt like this was the first step of my journey.

The first building I passed was the Reptile Zoo. From the outside, it looked like a rundown Cracker Barrel restaurant. I imagined inside there was a bunch of glass terrariums with dusty-eyed rattlesnakes and venom-mouthed Gila monsters. I wondered why we are so fascinated with things that can kill us. On another day, I probably would have stopped and paid the $7 to go inside because I like things like that. Always have.

I kept walking. Less than a block from the museum there was an old school bus that had been converted into a restaurant. It was called the Old School BBQ. McKale loved barbeque. *She would like that,* I thought.

About five miles outside the town of Monroe, I passed a small structure that some believer had built alongside the road. There was a weathered, painted sign out front that read in a fancy, dated script:

The Wayside Chapel
Pause, Rest, Worship.

The chapel was a shedlike edifice that had a steeple added to it. I crossed the road to look inside. There were brightly colored plastic flowers covered in mud in front of the doorway. I slowly opened the door in case someone might be inside, but it was vacant. On the front wall was a large, wooden cross made from stained two-by-fours. There were four pews, each big enough to fit two people.

I stepped inside and walked up to the front of the chapel. There were notes and letters left on the pulpit by passersby. There was also a stack of music CDs someone had left on the front pew: *Marvin Pious and the Holy Crooners—Make a Joyful Noise.* There was a picture of Marvin and his band, in matching orange polyester jumpsuits. Marvin's haircut would be best described as a cross between an '80s mullet and a Chia Pet. There was a large Bible, an aged, white leather book, fanned open to 2 Thessalonians:

> Now our Lord Jesus Christ himself, and God, even our Father, which hath loved us, and hath given us everlasting consolation and good hope through grace . . .

Good hope through grace, I thought. I closed the Bible. *Love and consolation?* In a sudden flash of anger, I threw the book against the wall. *Love, hope,* and *grace?* What a joke. I walked out of the place, wishing I hadn't stopped.

I walked nearly a mile before I felt calm again. But the anger was still there. The emotion had always been there, concealed beneath a thin veneer of civility. The chapel had just exposed it.

I turned my attention to the road. The highway straightened a little, and I could clearly see the mountains in the distance. They were white with clouds and snow pack. Trees jutted up through the snow-covered slopes like beard stubble. The mountain was my destination. *That's a really long way to walk,* I thought. I shook my head, amused by my stupidity. This was nothing compared to where I was going. Crossing the country, I'd face a half-dozen or so mountain passes that would make this one look like a pitcher's mound.

I had walked about 12 miles when I reached the town of Sultan. The only way into the town was over a narrow metal bridge with no pedestrian lane and cars screaming by at 50 miles per hour or more. I wasn't sure what to do. It looked like a sure way to get hit. For the record, I didn't fear dying. I feared *almost* dying. They're not the same thing.

I puzzled over what to do for a moment, then found a solution. There was another bridge running parallel to the highway bridge. A train bridge. There was no *almost* dying with a train. Trains don't swerve.

I climbed over to the bridge and began walking across, slowly picking my way between the heavy rusted rails and the wood trestles. The bridge was about 70 yards across, and travel across it was slow. Still, I reached the other side without the least excitement. I wondered if the track was even used anymore. Part of me was disappointed. I stepped off the tracks and walked into the town.

I stopped for lunch at a deli. I'm not sure that the deli even had a name, which, in retrospect, was probably a wise choice on their part. I ordered a ham and cheese sandwich and a Coke with a small tub of potato salad. Even as hungry as I was, I ate very little. The food was awful. This was one of those meals that if you had to choose between eating the food or razorblades, you would stop to weigh the pros and cons. Before I left the deli, I took out a Pop-Tart and then ate it as I walked.

The next town I came to was called Startup, a "blink

and you'll miss it" community that seemed to consist mostly of mobile homes and tall grass.

As Bill Bryson observed, American towns are usually named after "the first white person to arrive or the last Indian to leave." Here, I thought, was a welcome exception—a city council that had shown a little initiative. I was wrong. I learned the town name's origin from a plaque mounted near the gas station where I stopped to use the bathroom.

It turns out that the town was originally called Wallace, after the first white settler, but the post office kept sending the town's mail to Wallace, Idaho, so a vote was taken, and the name was officially changed to Startup, not after some hopeful ambition, rather after *George Startup*, manager of the Wallace Lumber Company. Bryson was wrong. City naming, like everything else in this world, is a function of money and politics.

The next town was Gold Bar, marked by a sign that declared itself *Gateway to the Cascades*. In the center of the town was a large totem pole and several coffee huts: The Coffee Coral, Let's Go Espresso, and Espresso Chalet.

As I walked through those small places, I couldn't help but wonder about their inhabitants. How they came to settle there and, more puzzling, why they stayed. Was it just because it's what they know? Is human nature really that clinging?

Gold Bar had a roadside church, slightly bigger than the one I had stopped at—Vitality Christian Church—a one-room shack with a large cross nailed to the outside wall. This time I had the sense to just keep walking.

Rain fell off and on during the day—not enough to stop my walking, but enough to soak the bottoms of my pants and keep me cold and miserable. I had walked about 20 miles and was thinking about making camp when I saw a sign for Zeke's Drive-in—home of world famous shakes.

It's a curious phenomenon that nearly all of these road-side stands had something they're supposedly world famous for. I wondered if it was just marketing hype or if something had actually happened to make the proprietor feel worthy of the claim.

Next to the drive-in was a red train caboose. As I drew near, I noticed the land behind it was marked with NO TRESPASSING signs. I decided to get some dinner and ask about nearby campsites.

The menu was hand painted on a sheet of plywood mounted to the outside wall. Zeke's had the usual drive-in fare except for one standout—the ostrich burger. Unlike me, McKale liked to try new things and probably would have ordered it.

A tall man with amber hair stood at the window watching me approach. The grill behind him was flaring with small grease fires. When I was ten feet from the window, he asked, "What can I get you?"

"What does an ostrich burger taste like?"

From the readiness of his pitch, I guessed he'd already been asked this ten thousand times. "Ostrich is popular. It's red meat, you know, just like beef, but leaner. Very lean. It's great for people who are watching their waistlines."

McKale *definitely* would have ordered it. My waistline wasn't much of a concern for me these days, but I was curious. "I'll have one of those," I said. "What's the difference between the regular ostrich burger and the deluxe ostrich burger?"

"Cheese and pickles," he said.

"I'll have the deluxe."

"You want French fries to go with that?"

"Sure."

He jotted this down with a stub of a pencil.

"And, I'd like one of your *world-famous* shakes." I stressed the words *world-famous*, as if adding quotation marks with my voice, but he didn't react.

"What kind?"

At least two-thirds of the menu was a listing of shakes and malts, with flavors ranging from banana caramel to grasshopper. In addition there were two seasonal specials, gingerbread and rhubarb. I asked which was better.

"That depends."

"On what?"

"On whether you prefer gingerbread or rhubarb."

Ask a dumb question. "I'll try the rhubarb."

"Good choice," he said. He rang up my order. I handed him a ten-dollar bill, and he gave me back some change and a receipt. "You're number thirty-four," he said, which I found mildly amusing since there was no one else waiting.

"Are these woods behind your restaurant yours?"

"No. I'm not sure who owns them. It's private property. One day the NO TRESPASSING signs just popped up."

"Would anyone hassle me if I camped back there?"

"Doubt it. Every now and then, I'll see someone crawl out of there in the morning. In fact, we had a fellow lived back there for more than a year. No one made a fuss about that. He wasn't shy about it, either. He built himself a little shack. I don't remember his name." He turned back to the girl at the grill. "What was that guy's name who lived in the woods back there?"

She said something, and he nodded, "Oh, yeah." He turned back. "His name was Itch. His father was a big-wig politician in Seattle. Lived back there for more than a year. Don't know why he chose that place. Just liked it, I guess. He'd walk up and down the highway and pick up people's lost change and aluminum cans, and when he had enough money, he'd come by and get something to eat. One day he just up and left. Haven't seen him since. So why do you ask?"

I'd forgotten what I'd asked. "Ask what?"

"About camping back there."

"I'm looking for a place to spend the night."

"Well, it's gonna rain on you." There was another flare-up behind him. "Where you from?"

"Seattle."

He looked me over a moment, then said, "You can sleep in the caboose."

I looked at the big red caboose. "That one right here?" Another stupid question.

"Only one I got. The mattresses aren't there anymore. But if you don't mind sleeping on wood."

"Thank you. The shelter would be appreciated."

Someone behind him shouted, "Number thirty-four!"

He turned around and carefully put my food in a sack, then handed it to me with the shake. "When you're done eating, just come back up, and I'll unlock the caboose for you."

"Thank you."

There was an enclosed dining area in a separate building behind the restaurant. The room was clean and held six picnic tables. The walls were covered with maps of area hiking trails, and there was an article about bear attacks. (The article was published by the local Chamber of Commerce, so it had a lot of good things to say about bears.)

I sat down at a table and unwrapped the wax paper from my ostrich burger. Ostrich meat may look like beef, but it isn't as good. I just put more ketchup on it.

It felt good to be off my feet. I hadn't changed my socks since the day before, and I felt as if my flesh was absorbing them. I looked forward to taking them off, though not yet. I was eating.

When I finished my meal, I cleaned up the table, then walked back out to the drive-in. Three cars were now parked out front, and a line had formed at the window. The man saw me and said, "Just hang tight for a minute. I'll have to unlock it for you." About twenty minutes later he emerged from a side door. "This way."

I followed him around back, then up a short set of stairs to the caboose. He pulled out a key ring and unlocked the door. Both of us stepped inside, standing in the narrow aisle that ran the length of the car. The interior of the caboose had been painted submarine gray and smelled like wet paint. "Don't use the head," he said. "It doesn't work, and you'd have a real mess on your hands. You can use the facilities behind the restaurant. I'll leave the door unlocked."

I was surprised at how trusting he was of a complete stranger.

"Thank you."

"Don't mention it."

He walked out, shutting the door behind himself. I had never actually been inside a train (unless you count the Park train at Disneyland), let alone slept in one. The berth was a long wooden tray where I suppose a mattress once lay. I laid out my pad, then unzipped my sleeping bag and lay it across the space. I lay back to test it out. Not bad. Hard, but I was getting used to that. For the most part, the soft things of my life were gone.

As night fell, the rain started coming down harder, and the sound was amplified by the wooden box I was sheltered in. I was glad to be inside.

I pulled the flashlight from my pack and my road journal and jotted down a few notes for the day. I wrote a little about the homeless man at the Jack in the Box and the teacher's book. I wondered if, in time, I would become like him—rambling about things others couldn't understand. *The teacher book.*

I hated the night and the demons that waited until dark to come out. Even though I thought about McKale all day and sometimes about Kyle or his treachery, there was some power in walking that kept my demons at bay. But in the silence and still of the night, they came out in legion. At such times, I felt like a stranger in my own mind, wandering through a mysterious and precarious landscape.

I think it was Twain who wrote, "I suppose I'm like the rest of humanity: not quite sane at night."

CHAPTER

Twenty-five

I spent the night sleeping in a train caboose. I can't imagine what the new day will bring except, of course, more walking. And more rain.

Alan Christoffersen's diary

The world was quiet when I woke. The dawn sun had not yet climbed over the mountain, and the world was still blue and gray. The air was cold enough that I could see my breath.

I packed up my things. It wasn't raining anymore, but the world outside was still wet, as if the rain had stopped just an hour or two earlier. I walked around to the back of the darkened drive-in and pushed on the bathroom door. I was glad when it opened.

I shaved with warm water, then filled my canteen with cold. I shrugged on my pack, then walked back out to the road.

The highway passed over a river, and below me there was a group of people unloading kayaks from a truck. No one was in a hurry. It occurred to me that neither was I. For the first time, I thought about the simplicity of my new life. No deadlines. No appointments or meetings. No e-mails or phone conferences. All I had to think about were the necessities—water, food, sleep, and occasional shelter.

The road was veiled in a haze, a cool mist that either rose from the asphalt or fell from the sky, I wasn't sure which. After a steep climb of a few miles, I saw water-falls cascading off the north side of the mountains. To the south of me was the Skykomish River. Even in my state of mind, I couldn't deny the beauty of this country.

Around ten, I entered the city of Baring, where I ate a simple but delicious breakfast of eggs and link sausage at a roadside diner. It was a quiet day, gray and morose. If the sky wasn't overcast I still would have been in shadow from the lush canopy of trees. The deep forest was green in moss and lichen, and even the concrete rails of the bridges were flocked with moss.

At Moneycreek campground, I stopped to rest and eat an apple, jerky, and a couple handfuls of trail mix.

The road had become more narrow and dangerous. Compounding the problem was that this city did not tolerate slow drivers. It's the only place I had ever seen with signs threatening drivers with tickets if they had more than five cars trailing behind them. The offered solution was "shoulder driving," an obvious hazard for bikers and hikers. Baring wasn't a place to be walking after dusk. At least if you wanted to live.

In Skykomish, I stopped at the only place I could find to eat lunch, the Sky Deli. The next town was farther than I could reasonably walk, so I resigned myself to my last hot meal for the day. I ordered spaghetti with raguot and garlic bread. I let the food settle a bit, then headed back out to the road.

By mile marker 56, I had walked nearly 25 miles, almost all of it uphill, which became obvious even without the elevation signs that were now posted at regular intervals. I could feel it in my calves. The first of the elevation signs was at 1,500 feet where, for the first time, I encountered snow on the road.

By dusk, my legs were cramping, and I started looking in earnest for a place to camp. There were few possibilities, as the road was surrounded by steep terrain on both sides. An hour later, I seriously wondered how much farther I could walk and scolded myself for not stopping earlier. I even considered walking back 7 miles to where I saw the last campsite, but the thought of losing those hard-earned miles was too painful, so I just trudged ahead, hoping for something.

In the next mile, the elevation rose to 1,800 feet, a 300-foot climb evidenced by the increasing amount of snow on the mountain and shoulders. My thighs and calves were burning, while my breath froze in front of me. I was near my limit when, through the dark, I saw a sign for Deception Falls campground. I was filled with relief.

I crossed the street to the camp, stepping over the chain pulled across the entrance. The site was closed for the season. There were NO CAMPING signs posted in the parking lot, but this did nothing to deter me. My legs were gone. I had no choice but to stop.

The public outhouses were locked. I followed a cut trail down into a dark, wet valley. The river and falls roared loud enough to drown out the sound of the highway. The foliage was thick and green, accented with occasional patches of snow. It seemed as if moss coated everything, and I was certain that if I stayed there long enough, the ecosystem would claim me as well.

The falls were not high but strong, a collusion of violent, mountain-borne waters falling 100 feet or more in a series of sharp rocky inclines. According to the engraved wooden park sign, the waters pounded down with seven tons of force. At the bottom of the sign was a quote:

> "There is nothing as weak as water, but when it attacks and is persistent, nothing can withstand it."
> —Lao Tse

Beneath that quote were the handwritten words:

> All waterfalls are temporary. One day all this will be worn away, and the flow of water will just transition smoothly from one place to another. All things pass with time.

Everyone's a philosopher, I thought. The words may have been true, but it wasn't going to change in my lifetime.

There were more NO CAMPING signs on the trail below. That time of the year, the public was not even supposed to be hiking there. I doubted that the Park Service patrolled these places so late in the season, but in case they did, I found a flat piece of ground, hidden from the trail, to construct my tent. It was dark by the time I finished.

The air was considerably warmer inside my tent, but the sound of the water was only slightly dulled. I laid out my pad and sleeping bag, then pulled off my shoes and socks to let my feet breathe. The crash of the falls drowned out not only the occasional car on the highway above but my thoughts as well. For the first time in days, I slept soundly.

CHAPTER

Twenty-six

I ran into an old friend today. At least someone I mistook for a friend. Judas-Ralph. Traitors are the lowliest of God's creatures, despised by those they betray and secretly loathed by those whom they serve.

Alan Christoffersen's diary

I woke to strange voices. They were not speaking English. German or Lithuanian perhaps. (I don't know why I thought that. I have no idea what Lithuanian sounds like.) Whatever the dialect, the voices were soon gone.

My legs were deservedly sore, and I stretched them as far as my sleeping bag would permit.

The air was cold enough that I could see my breath, which had condensed on the pitched vinyl roof of my tent in a plane of pregnant drops. As I sat up, I brushed the side of the tent, which brought down a shower of freezing droplets.

I opened my pack and lifted out my water and Pop-Tarts. I was famished and ate two full packages, four pastries in all. I reminded myself of Tolkien's Hobbits, eating their elven lembas bread. Only my staple was Pop-Tarts. For the first time I wished I had brought something else.

I put on my parka, hat, and gloves, then climbed out of the tent. I walked to the edge of the water to shave, but it was freezing, so I prudently decided that one day's growth wasn't going to harm anyone.

I collapsed my tent and was packed up in just a matter of minutes. Even with sore legs, I was eager to get going. According to my map, Stevens Pass was about 8 miles up the road. There would be facilities there—a lodge, restrooms, and restaurant. I was looking forward to stopping for some warm food and comfort, then crossing over to the other side of the mountain. The downhill side.

I climbed up out of the campground, threw away some trash in the camp's garbage cans—empty water bottles and wrappers—then walked back out to the road, crossing over the falls that passed beneath.

In the morning light, I could clearly see the mountain rising ahead of me, white and silent. I was in its lap. My pack felt heavier than the day before, though I knew it wasn't. I was just worn out.

In the next 3 miles, the road climbed to 2,600 feet, and the shoulders of the road were completely covered in snow, though fortunately the snowplows had pushed it back from the bike lane. My taupe hiking boots were stained dark umber, but they were dry inside (except for my sweat), and I was glad that I had taken the time to properly waterproof them.

After another hour of walking, I saw there was more than a foot of snow on the shoulders. I could tell I was getting closer to the summit as most of the cars that passed me were loaded down with skis and tubes. A man on foot looked ridiculously out of place.

There was a rise of another 1,000 feet between the falls and Stevens Pass—which is both the name of the mountain pass and the ski resort perched at its peak. I arrived by mid-morning. The sign outside the resort placed the elevation at 4,061 feet. In the past two days, I had climbed more than 2,500 feet.

The resort was crowded, and the snow-packed parking

lot north of the highway was filled nearly to capacity with traffic waiting on both sides of the street to enter.

I fell in with the bustling skiers and walked up to the lodge. The building was crowded with people milling about in brightly colored parkas and ski caps. I was no longer bothered by the crowds, though I felt no sense of belonging either.

I slid my pack off my shoulders and carried it inside the lodge. The first thing I did was use the resort's restroom, which under the circumstance was an unspeakable luxury. Especially the hot water. I didn't shave. The men's room was too busy for that. But I took my time washing my hands and face in the warm water. Afterwards, I went to the restaurant to get something to eat.

The dining room was already crowded for lunch. I found a small, unoccupied table near the front window and laid claim to it with my pack. Then I went up to the counter where I grabbed a plastic tray, then ordered a large hot chocolate, a glazed donut, a double chili cheese-burger, and an extra-large order of cheese fries. The food was expensive compared to what I had been paying, and for the first time I used my debit card. I was happy that they accepted it as I had no idea how much money was in my account.

I carried my food back to the table and devoured it. When I finished eating, I got myself another tall hot choc-olate and an apple fritter. For the first time in my life such gluttony brought no guilt. I was steadily losing weight and would probably burn the calories off before dinner.

I took off my parka and hung it over the back of my

chair, then just sat, dunking the fritter in my cocoa and taking in the ambience. I wondered why McKale and I had never come here before.

At the table behind me, a pair of stylishly outfitted yuppie parents was trying to talk their little girl into going back out to ski. She didn't want to and wasn't shy about telling them or anyone else in the dining room. The room's occupancy and noise level was such that hardly anyone paid attention to her screaming. The couple was helpless. They first bribed her with a Hello Kitty parka but quickly upped the ante with a karaoke machine, then, pulling out the big guns, went right for the puppy, but she was already out of control (though clearly in control of her parents) and past appeasement.

While I was musing over their dilemma, a short, bowling pin–shaped man with his ski bib pulled down to his waist waddled into the dining room. Something was familiar about his walk and shape. When he removed his ski goggles, my chest constricted. I immediately recognized the bright red hair and thin lips. (And ferretlike face.) It was Ralph, my former head of design and Kyle's new partner.

He sat down only three tables away from mine where his wife and children were already eating. They were situated near the front door, and I had probably walked right by them on my way in. I was surprised that I hadn't recognized his wife, Cheryl, but even more so that she was with him. Over the last year, I'd rarely seen them together, in part because she had no apparent interest in his occupation, or him, but more likely because he was having an affair with a woman he met a year earlier at a graphics convention. I don't know why his betrayal of me surprised me. Cheaters cheat. If he'd cheat on his wife, why should I assume he'd be loyal to me?

Anger warmed through me. I considered either punching him out or telling him off, and preferably both. But as I watched him interact with his wife and children, I decided against either. I was already treading water in an ocean of emotion, and an embarrassing showdown in front of his wife and kids—no matter how much he deserved it—would not really make me feel better.

I took my Ray-Bans from my pack and slid them on, pulled down the brim of my hat, and became invisible. As I sipped my hot chocolate, both Ralph and Cheryl looked my way several times, but neither recognized me. Dressed like this, and with my furry face, I could be Brad Pitt and not be recognized.

Unfortunately, sitting that close to Ralph ruined my stay. I finished my cocoa, then put my parka back on and lifted my pack up over my shoulder. As I approached Ralph's table, I heard him say to his oldest son, Eric, "Where did you get that thing?"

Eric, a straw-blond twelve-year-old, was playing with some kind of a radio and looked up defiantly. "Nowhere. Someone left it on that table."

"Well, put it back," Ralph said. "It's not yours."

"Take it easy," Cheryl said. "He just found it."

"I don't care. It's not his."

The irony was too great to pass up. It was as if fate had handed me the assist. "He's right," I said to Eric. "You don't want to take something that doesn't belong to you. That would be wrong." I looked at Ralph. "Wouldn't it?"

Ralph and Cheryl looked at me, blinking with surprise. "Excuse me?" Ralph said.

"No, I won't." I leaned forward. "Remember, Ralphie, whether it's Cheryl or me you're cheating on, it's all the same. The reward for cheating is you end up in bed with a cheater."

I turned and walked out of the lodge, sure that Ralph's eyes were glued to my back. He probably had figured out who I was, but I was the least of his problems now. At least he and Cheryl would finally have something to talk about.

The air braced my skin as I walked back outside and down to the road. The east side of the pass was all downhill, a decided advantage for hiking, except for the fact that the walking conditions on that side of the mountain were less favorable, and snow covered the lines marking the bike lane. I wasn't sure if it was the eastern winds that had caused the unfavorable conditions on one side of the mountain, but the pass was the dividing line between King and Chelan County, so politics might have had more to do with it than weather. Even with the traction of my boots, I found the road slippery, and as I left the resort, I slipped and fell in front of a line of cars, which was more embarrassing than painful, and I hoped that Ralph wasn't watching. I almost fell two other times, and I began mentally drafting a strongly worded complaint to the county roads department.

Fortunately, by late afternoon, the elevation had fallen to 2,800 feet, and the snow was considerably diminished on the road, gathered only in occasional crusted patches that I just stepped over.

My thoughts kept wandering back to my Ralph encounter. I wondered if Cheryl already knew he was cheating. I didn't regret saying what I did. Revenge, they say, is a dish best served cold. I have no idea what that means, but it seemed especially apropos for a ski resort. At any rate, I could have done much worse.

At twilight, an Acura MDX that was headed down the mountain slowed down next to me and a blond teenage girl leaned out the passenger window. "Want a ride?" she asked. I guessed she'd been drinking. Coldplay blared from their stereo.

"No thank you."

"Where you going?"

"Florida."

"Where is he going?" the driver asked. She was also a teenage girl. I hoped she hadn't been drinking. Just then a car pulled up behind their car, honked, then swerved around them.

"He said Florida," the window blonde said.

The driver said something I couldn't hear. Then the girl leaned back out the window. "We'll drive you."

"Thanks. I'd rather walk."

She laughed. "Have fun."

The car sped off.

After two more miles, there was no more snow on the road or shoulders, which I was especially pleased about since it was time to make camp. According to my map, there was a town ahead, but I wasn't sure how far or how big it was, or even if there would be any place to stay. I hoped there would be. I was chilled to the core and desperately wanted a warm bath and a place to wash my sweat-stained clothes.

In spite of the time I spent lingering at the pass, I had covered a lot of ground—the most of any day so far— nearly 30 miles. My legs were okay, except my knees hurt a little from walking downhill.

As I came around a gradual bend in the road, I saw something set back through the trees. There was an un- paved, gravel pull-off, and not far behind it was a col- lection of dilapidated yellow shacks. They looked like they may have once been one-room rentals for skiers, but they had obviously been deserted for many years. One of the shacks was completely collapsed, the roof now lying on the ground, its asphalt-tile roof covered in moss and leaves. The other structures were in varying degrees of disrepair.

There was something about the place that made me anxious, and as I approached the first shack, I had the sud- den macabre thought that I might find something inside that I didn't want to see. I suppose it reminded me of the kind of place serial killers hid things in True Crime stories. I didn't know what made me think of that.

I looked inside the first structure. There were no bod- ies, but it was clear that I wasn't the first human to find the place. The interior was a man-sized rat's nest. The room was filled with some bizarre junk—drained beer bottles, a molded mattress, an army jacket, the back seat of a Ford Pinto, a purple brassiere, empty plastic antifreeze bottles, and shredded newspapers.

I checked out the other shacks. They also had wood floors likewise heaped with their own eclectic contributions from past occupants. Two of them still had remnants of the original carpet—rotted and spotted black with mold like a leopard's hide.

The windows were all broken out of them, and they offered only a little shelter, but there is something about a roof overhead that makes one feel more secure.

The shack I settled on was structurally the most sound of the four and had a fireplace that was still intact. I inspected the hearth and chimney, then gathered wood from one of the fallen structures and started a fire. The hearth was filled with wet leaves, and the chimney was partially clogged, so smoke backed up inside the room, which wasn't much of a problem, since there were holes in the roof and walls.

The flame was a thing of beauty as the shack filled with heat and light. I wondered if anyone would notice the fire at night, but I didn't worry about it. People driving by were going somewhere. They didn't have time to care about such things.

I laid out my pad and sleeping bag, then rooted through my pack for dinner. There wasn't much left to eat—an apple, jerky, trail mix, and two energy bars. I should have bought something at the resort; I had planned to, but I was in a bit of a hurry to leave. I finished off the trail mix and jerky, then sat back and slowly ate my apple.

I had accomplished a victory of sorts. The snow and mountain had worried me more than I let on to myself, but it hadn't really been that big a deal. I wanted to tell someone what I had accomplished, but there was no one who would want to hear. McKale would have wanted to know all about it.

I threw the apple core into the fire, then crawled into my bag to sleep.

CHAPTER

Twenty-seven

It happened again. Sometimes the most frightening place to be is in our own skin.

Alan Christoffersen's diary

I woke in the night at the sound of hail. It was an impressive storm, and even with the dense tree cover overhead, it sounded like a hundred ball-peen hammers pounding on the shack's roof. Marble-sized ice balls flew in through the window and popped off the floor like popcorn, gathering in one corner in frozen white piles. The fire was smoldering, its embers glowing and occasionally hissing from the hail. I considered starting the fire up again but decided against it. It was too cold to leave my bag.

Suddenly my body turned on me. My chest and throat constricted, my skin flushed, and my heart began to race. This wasn't the first time I had had a panic attack. It happened a lot when I was a boy in the months following my mother's death. I never told my father about it. McKale was the only one who ever knew. She was the only one who had ever comforted me through it. Now it was happening because of her. Or lack of her.

I sat there for several minutes, trembling. I reached down the front of my shirt and grasped the ring that hung from the chain around my neck.

Then, in the dark, I groped through my backpack until I found McKale's camisole. I pulled it out and buried my face in it. Through the silk fabric I shouted, "Why did you leave me! Why did you make me promise to live?"

There was no answer but the pounding hail. I pulled my sleeping bag up over my head and tried to go back to sleep. I couldn't stop shaking.

I don't remember falling asleep, but I woke at daybreak. The hail had stopped, replaced by heavy rainfall. I sat up. My back hurt from the hard floor. I climbed out of my bag, and for a few minutes I just sat, listening to the rain, watching a steady stream of water cascade down the east wall and pool near the fireplace. My chest still ached from the night before.

For the first time, I wished I had my cell phone. I felt lonely. I wanted someone to talk to. I wasn't particular. Anyone who would listen.

It wasn't just my back and chest that hurt. My whole body ached, but I wasn't sore from walking, and I wasn't sick. At least not physically.

I looked out at the rain and sighed. I had no desire to walk. The only thing more painful would be to sit inside a dank, molding box and think.

I was also nearly out of food. I rooted through my backpack and brought out the energy bars. I took one of them, peeled back the wrapper, and ate it. Then I ate the second one, depleting the last of my food. I threw the wrappers on the floor—my contribution to the nest. There was no need to douse the fire. The rain had already taken care of that.

I pulled my poncho on over my parka, put on my hat,

flung my backpack over my shoulder, and walked out into the storm. The forest floor was muddy and dark, and torn strips of green leaves littered the ground, shredded from the night's hail.

As I left the protection of the trees' canopy, the rain loudly bounced off my hat and poncho. I truly loved my hat. It was one thing that made me happy. I could imagine the Aussies in the outback, herding sheep or kangaroos or whatever in their Akubra hats, the rain spitting down on them, rolling off their hats' brims to their shoulders. The more it rained the more I loved my hat. I wondered if I would look ridiculous wearing it in Key West.

The traffic was light, whether because it was still early or because everyone else was smarter than me and stayed inside, I don't know. The road still gradually descended, though not as much as the first few miles from the pass. I was glad for this, as not just my spirit was resistant to walking, but my body as well. I felt like I was forcing every step. I hoped there was something in the next town.

Ninety minutes later I spotted a building. The 59er Diner—a relatively ambitious establishment for a gas-stop town—was a fifties' style building with bright pink streamers and a neon sign that proclaimed WORLD FAMOUS SHAKES. I was deliriously happy to see it.

To the east of the building was a small side yard with a healthy grass lawn and a wood fence as eclectically deco-rated as a yard sale. There were old bicycles and red Radio

Flyer wagons, a parking meter, pink flamingos, and a set of drive-in movie speakers.

Behind the yard was a row of small bungalows brightly painted and clean, about twice the size of the shack where I had spent the night and probably not unlike what it looked like a decade or two ago.

I walked up to the restaurant. I held the door while three women exited, then stepped inside to the warmth and the pleasing smell of ice cream and pancake batter. The interior of the building was loud and cluttered with fifties relics. There was a vintage neon-lit jukebox playing vinyl 45s—Elvis's "Jailhouse Rock"—and a soda counter with chrome-stemmed, vinyl bar stools.

This place was serious about their claim of world-famous shakes. There was a whiteboard with the number of shakes served that year, 23,429 so far, with an appeal to help them break their annual record of 27,462.

A tall, flaxen-haired woman approached me. She wore a pink apron and a name tag that read BETTY SUE. "Nice hat," she said. "Just you, honey?"

"Yes, ma'am."

"Right this way."

She led me to a round, laminate-topped table in the back of the restaurant. "How's this?"

"Just great. Thank you."

"Your waitress will be right with you."

I took off my pack and leaned it against the wall, then removed my hat and poncho. I set my hat on the table, rolled up the poncho and stowed it in my pack, then sat down. The walls were decorated in a fifties collage of old license plates, *Life* magazine covers, Elvis paraphernalia, record covers, antique Coca-Cola and Pepsi signs, and pinups of fifties stars: Marilyn Monroe, Marlon Brando, James Dean, and Lucille Ball.

There were also printed advertisements from the fifties, including one for an iron that promised to iron 30 percent faster (and so many women are using them!), and another for cool compresses for "tired eyes."

Mounted on the wall above me was a small black-and-white television playing *The Three Stooges*. I decided that I truly was impressed with the work that had gone into the place, and not just because I'd spent the night in a landfill.

I pulled a menu from the chrome table stand and looked over their breakfast offerings. Banana pancakes with two eggs just $2.99. Biscuits and gravy $3.49. Everything looked good.

Just then my waitress arrived. She was a little over five feet, thin and didn't quite fill out the jeans she was wearing. She had long brown hair pulled back into a ponytail and dark, almond-shaped eyes. She looked at me as if she recognized me.

"Hello. Nice hat."

"Thank you."

"I'm Flo." Her introduction was redundant as her name was amply displayed on the license plate–sized name tag on her chest.

"Flo," I repeated. "What's your real name?"

She smiled. "You know, in the three years I've been here, you're the first to ask. It's Ally."

"Nice to meet you, Ally."

She rested her hands on her hips, then asked, "Are you okay?"

I was surprised by her question. "Sure. A little wet. A lot wet. But I'm fine."

She nodded. "Okay. Are you ready to order?"

"Yes. I'll have the banana pancakes and biscuits and gravy."

"Hungry," she said as she wrote it down. "Hungry and soggy. Anything to drink?"

"Orange juice and some hot chocolate."

"Orange juice. Hot cocoa," she said. "Be right back." She spun around and walked away. She returned a minute later with a mug. There was a cloud of cream about half as tall as the cup. "There you are. I hope you wanted whipped cream on your cocoa. I went a little crazy with it. I'll scoop it off if you don't."

"I like whipped cream," I said.

"Good."

"Do you know anything about those bungalows out back?"

"Yes. What do you want to know?"

"Are there any vacancies?"

"I'm sure there are."

"How much are they?"

"About a hundred dollars a night."

"Do they have hot water?"

She smiled. "Well, of course they do. They're just like little hotel rooms."

"How do I rent one?"

"I'll get you a flier."

She walked back through a set of swinging doors, then returned with a small, color-copy sales piece. Like the diner, the bungalows were themed. There was a western motif, a tropical island paradise, and the Big Bopper, which looked like an extension of the diner.

"They're all vacant. It's $98 a night," she said. "But I'm sure I could get you a deal."

"Thank you."

Ally stepped back from the table. "And your breakfast should be out real soon."

She returned a few minutes later holding a large platter with a hot pad. "Here you are. Be careful, the plate's hot."

The tall, lightly browned biscuits were covered with gravy and garnished with parsley flakes and paprika. As she set the plate down, I noticed two thick scars running horizontally across her right wrist. She caught me looking and quickly withdrew her arm, laying it to her side.

"I talked with the owner," she said. "He says he'll rent you a bungalow for just $59 a night. And you can occupy it immediately."

"Thank you. I'd like that."

"When you're done eating, I'll take you through them. Do you need anything else?"

I looked over the table. "My juice."

"Of course. Sorry." She ran back, then returned with a tall glass of orange juice. She handed it to me with her left hand. "That's on me. Enjoy your meal."

"Thank you."

The food was delicious. The biscuits and gravy were especially good. When I finished eating, Ally returned with my bill.

"Anything else?"

"No, I'm good." I gave her my debit card.

"I'll ring this up then show you the bungalows."

A moment later, she returned with my card, the check, and three room keys attached to wooden key chains roughly the size of boat paddles. On each key chain was printed the name of one of the bungalows.

I signed the check, then put on my hat, lifted my pack and followed her out the back door.

The first bungalow she took me to had a tropical decor. The walls were brightly painted with island foliage, exotic birds, parrots, and cockatiels. I wasn't particular about where I stayed and said so, but Ally insisted on showing me her favorite—the Big Bopper. "I think this is the nicest of the three," she said unlocking the door.

The interior was clean and painted robin's egg blue, the same color as a Tiffany's gift box. The walls were covered with pictures from the fifties: Sinatra, Brando, Elvis, but predominantly of Marilyn Monroe, which included a large poster of her kneeling on a bed. The front room had a black-and-white checkered tile landing, a couch, and a television.

The kitchen was small, crowded with a microwave oven, a small laminate table with two chrome-back chairs, a small refrigerator, an electric fan, and a porcelain sink with two pink fuzzy dice hanging from the ceiling above it. The bathroom had a shower bath with plastic shower

curtains printed with pictures of silhouetted girls in poo-
dle skirts.

"This is perfect," I said. I laid my pack against the front
wall. "I'll take it."

"Don't you want to see the Western bungalow?"

"No, you said this is your favorite. I'll take your word
for it."

"Here's your key." She walked to the front door. "I work
until seven tonight, so if you need anything, you know
where to find me."

"Thank you."

"You are very welcome. Have a nice stay."

She stepped outside, and I shut the door behind her.

The first thing I did was dump the contents of my backpack in a pile on the floor of the front room. Everything I
had was filthy, damp, and smelled. I filled the tub with hot
water, then dropped in all my clothes, including the ones
I was wearing. I kneeled down and hand washed them all
with shampoo. The water turned the color of weak coffee. When I had washed everything, I emptied the water
from the tub then refilled it with fresh, scalding hot water
and let my clothes soak. I wrapped a towel around myself,
then opened the front door and shook out my pack, emp-
tying it of crumbs, trail mix, and dirt.

I went back to the tub, unstopped the drain, and, piece
by piece, pulled my clothes from the water, wrung them
out by hand, then hung them to dry over whatever I could
find: chair backs, the sofa, towel bars, the bed's headboard.
I hung the clothes I needed first in the kitchen next to the
fan. I considered putting my cargo pants in the microwave

to dry them but decided against it. The last thing I needed was a fire.

I got a fresh razor from my hygiene bag, then went back to the bathroom. I turned on the shower until steam rose, then I climbed in myself, pulling the shower curtain closed. The sensation was remarkably luxurious, standing there, the hot water coursing over my body, a stream of dirty water running to the drain. I lathered soap over my face and neck and shaved. Then I scrubbed myself with soap and a washcloth.

When my body was clean, I plugged the drain, then ran the water until the tub was full, and lay back in it, placing the washcloth over my eyes. I lay there for nearly an hour, relaxing my sore muscles and joints, as well as my mind. When I finally emerged, I felt new again.

I dried myself off, then checked the clothes I'd hung by the fan. They were mostly dry, except my pants waist-band, which I took a hair dryer to.

After I was dressed, I walked back to the diner to get some lunch. It was around two and the diner was busy. Ally was up front and smiled when she saw me. "How's your room?"

"It's good. I took a bath."

"That's always a good thing. Looks like you shaved as well. Here, come sit over here." She led me to a booth up front and handed me a menu from the table. "Do you know what you want, or do you need a minute?"

I looked over the menu. "What's this Elvis Burger?"

"It's like a normal hamburger except with peanut butter and banana."

"You're kidding, right?"

"I am. It's just . . . meaty. I think it's like a half pound of beef—and it comes with fries and a big dill pickle."

"Meaty is good. How about that and some of your world famous blueberry cobbler."

"Very good choice. Anything to drink?"

"Just water."

"Water it is."

Fifteen minutes later, she brought back my food. There was also a large plate of French fries. "That's on me." She touched my shoulder. "Just holler if you need anything else."

"Thanks." As I ate, the diner was besieged by a busload of Amazon, sport uniform–wearing women. They looked like a volleyball team. Ally hopped from table to table like a bee on an azalea bush. I finished eating, then just sat and waited for her return. I was perfectly content to be in no hurry. Finally, Ally came over with my check. "Sorry that took so long. Those buses pull up, and *Katie bar the door.*"

I laughed at the idiom. "No worries. You earn your salary."

"Salary nothing. I live on tips. And these college kids are notoriously bad tippers. Last week someone left me a golf ball. Would you like anything else?"

"Yes." I took some money out of my wallet and put it with my check, sure to leave a generous tip. "I want to ask you something."

She looked at me curiously. "All right."

"Why did you ask if I was okay?"

Her brow furrowed. "I don't know. I just felt like something was wrong. Was I wrong?"

"No."

"*Are* you okay?"

I shook my head. "No."

She looked at me thoughtfully. Then she said, "I get off around seven. If you're not too busy, I'll bring dinner to your bungalow, and we can talk." Then she added, "It's okay if you want to be left alone, I understand. But if you'd like some company . . ."

"I'd like some company," I said.

"Then I'll come by around seven. Sometimes I'm a little later. It depends on how busy we are." She lifted the check. "Pray for no buses."

"I'll do that. Keep the change," I said.

"Thank you." She smiled, then walked back to the kitchen.

I went back to the bungalow. I checked my clothes. They were all still damp, so I turned the thermostat up five degrees. I took out my road diary and wrote a little, then laid back on the bed and watched the ceiling fan slowly turn until I fell asleep.

The room was dark when I woke to knocking. I sat up and looked around, momentarily forgetting where I was. There came another knock. I turned on a lamp, then walked to the door and opened it. Ally stood outside, clutching two paper sacks in one hand and holding two malts against her body. She had changed from her waitress outfit and wore a form-fitting sweater and jeans.

"Did I wake you?"

"No, I was just . . ." I grinned. "I was sleeping. Come in."

"Thank you." She walked directly to the kitchen, talking to me as she did. "I brought some sandwiches—our Spanky's Clubhouse, that's a triple decker with turkey, ham, bacon, cheese, and the meatloaf sandwich. Dan makes great meatloaf. You can take either sandwich. I also brought a taco baked potato, a basket of onion rings, and, of course, our world-famous chocolate-chocolate malt with extra malt."

She set the sacks on the kitchen table and put the malts in the refrigerator. "Are you ready to eat?"

"Yes . . . ," I said looking at the white briefs draped over the back of the kitchen chairs, "but I should probably get rid of these."

She smiled. "Not on my account . . ."

I gathered up my underwear, then pulled out one of the chairs. "Have a seat."

"Thank you."

I threw my underwear on the bed, then came back and sat down next to her at the table.

"At least now I won't have to ask boxers or briefs," she said.

"I'm glad we got that out of the way," I said.

She took the food from the sacks and laid it out across the table.

"You brought enough for a small village."

"We don't have to eat it all," she said, arranging metal utensils in front of me with the efficiency of a waitress. "I hate eating with plastic utensils," she said. "How about we share the sandwiches?"

"I'm good with that."

She had already cut the sandwiches in half and she handed me one of each. They were both good. "So, you did your wash."

"Yeah, I just hope everything dries before I have to leave. I thought of drying things in the microwave."

This made her smile. "Bad idea," she said. "So, the room's okay?"

"It's the Four Seasons compared to where I slept last night."

"And where was that?"

"About 5 miles up the mountain. I found these little shacks."

She said with food still in her mouth, "I know what you're talking about. There are four or five of them. One of them fell over."

"That's them."

"In the summer the teenagers around here go up there to party."

I took a bite of the meatloaf sandwich. "So you're from here?"

"No. I'm from Dallas."

"How does one go from Dallas to the 59er Diner?"

"I had a boyfriend who moved here to refurbish his aunt's cabin, and I followed him." She frowned. "Then he ran off with someone else."

"And left you here?"

"It's not like I'm chained here. I like it. At least for now. No one stays here forever. Except Dan."

"Who's Dan?"

"He owns the diner." She dipped an onion ring in ketchup. "You have beautiful eyes," she said. "Sad, but beautiful."

"Thank you."

"You're welcome. Where are you from?"

"Seattle, most recently."

She took a bite. "And less recently?"

"I was born in Colorado, raised in Pasadena."

"I spent a summer in Boulder, Colorado. I did a lot of hiking. It was fun. How long have you been on the road?"

"Not long. Five, six days."

"Where are you going?"

"Away."

She nodded. "That's a little . . . *vague*."

"When I left Bellevue, I decided to walk as far away as I could on the continent, which happens to be Key West, Florida."

"You're walking to Key West?"

"Yes."

"Wow. How many miles is that?"

"Three thousand something."

She thought this over. "I admire you. I think most people dream of doing something like that but never do. Life has too many shackles. So how does one just leave everything like that? You must have had a job, friends, family."

"I did."

"You mean until you left?"

"No, you might say they left me."

She nodded as if she suddenly understood. "Do you want to talk about it?"

To my surprise I did. "Classic riches to rags story. I had the perfect life. And in less than six weeks it was gone."

"So what did you do in that perfect life?"

"I owned a Seattle advertising agency." My voice softened, "Actually, money was only a small part of it. One day my wife was thrown from a horse. She was paralyzed from the chest down. Then a month later, she died from complications. While I was taking care of her, my business partner stole my agency, and my home went into foreclosure. I lost everything. That's when I decided to walk away."

"You stayed with your wife through it all."

I nodded. "Of course."

"That's really cool. I'm sorry about your wife. That must be so painful." I nodded. "And I'm sorry about your scumbag business partner. There's a special place in hell for people like him."

"So I've heard."

We ate in silence, letting the intensity of our conversation settle. She looked at my nearly empty plate. "Would you like your malt?"

"Sure."

She retrieved both cups from the refrigerator, then returned to her seat, setting a cup in front of me. "There's one upside to your adventure. With all that walking, you can probably eat whatever you want."

"I figure I burn about five thousand calories a day. Probably the same amount of calories this world-famous malt has."

She grinned. "I made this one myself. It's worth it. Trust me."

I lifted a spoon. "So how long do you plan to live here?"

"I actually don't live here, I live down the road in Peshastin. But, I don't know. Another year or two. I guess I'm just waiting."

"For what?"

She shrugged. "A better offer." She ate another spoonful of malt, then said, "How about you? Leaving in the morning?"

"I plan on it. What's the next big town?"

"It's still Leavenworth, just the city center. About 20 miles on. Have you ever been there?"

"No."

"You would remember if you had. It's a tourist attraction."

"What kind of attraction?"

"Leavenworth used to be a logging town. But when the sawmill shut down, the town almost died. Then someone had this idea to turn the town into a Bavarian hamlet."

"A what?"

"A Bavarian hamlet. A little slice of Germany in the middle of Washington. Now you can't sneeze if it's not in German. They claim to have the largest Oktoberfest celebration outside Munich. Too bad, you just missed it."

"Poor timing," I said, glad that I had missed it.

"At any rate, their plan worked. Today the town attracts millions of visitors a year. They have a city center, parks, and—point of interest—the world's largest nutcracker museum. It has, like, five thousand different nutcrackers."

"I'll have to check it out," I said.

"I'm sure you will," she said facetiously. "You know, it's kind of ironic, but if everything hadn't gone wrong with the town, they wouldn't be as well off as they are today. It just goes to show you that not all bad things are really bad." She took another spoonful of her malt. "You must be tired from all that walking."

"A little. Climbing Stevens Pass in the snow wasn't easy."

"I bet. How are your feet?"

"Sore."

"Come here." She stood, took my hand, and led me to the sofa. "Sit," she said. I sat down, and she sat cross-legged on the floor in front of me and untied my shoes.

"You sure you want to do that?" I asked.

"Absolutely. If you don't mind, that is."

"I won't stop you."

She pulled off my shoes, then began to gently knead my feet.

"Tell me if I'm doing it too hard or too soft."

"It's just right," I said.

For several moments, we both sat in silence. I couldn't believe how good it felt to be touched. I laid my head back and closed my eyes.

"Tell me about yourself," she said.

"I just did."

"That was your former self. No one goes through all you went through without changing."

I opened my eyes. "What do you want to know?"

"The real stuff. Like, what are you going to do when you reach Key West?"

"I don't know. Maybe just keep walking into the sea."

"Don't do that," she said.

"What else do you want to know?"

She thought for a moment. "Do you believe in God?"

"There's a question," I said.

"Does it have an answer?"

"Let's just say I'm much too angry at Him not to."

"You blame God for what happened to you?"

"Maybe. Probably."

She frowned, and I could tell that what I said had bothered her. "I didn't mean to offend you."

"You didn't. I just wonder why it is that we blame God for everything except the good. Did you blame Him for giving her to you in the first place? How many people go their whole lives and never get to experience that kind of love?"

I looked down.

"I'm not saying that you don't have the right to be angry. Life is tough." From her tone, I could tell there was more to what she said than she let on. I remembered her scars.

"Do you mind me asking what happened to your wrist?"

She stopped rubbing my feet. She looked down for a moment, and when she looked back up at me, there was strength in her eyes I hadn't seen before. "Well, like I said," she said softly, "life is tough.

"My stepfather sexually abused me from the age of seven until I was twelve, when I decided the only way out was to slit my wrist. I didn't know how to do it right, so I mostly just bled a lot while a neighbor girl called 911.

"At the hospital, a social worker got out of me why I had cut myself. My stepfather ended up going to prison for seven years. My mother blamed me for the whole situation. She accused me of seducing him, and she disowned me. So, at the age of thirteen, I was sent to the first of many foster homes. At fifteen, I ran away from my sixth foster placement with my nineteen-year-old boyfriend, who one day got tired of me and left.

"I lived on the streets of Dallas for almost a year until I was caught shoplifting at a Walmart and was sent to the Dallas County Juvenile Detention Center for three months.

"That's where I met Leah. Leah wasn't a juvie, she was older. She was one of the community volunteers. She became my friend and mentor. When I got out, she wanted me to go live with her, but I only promised to stay one week. But she was so good to me, I kept adding weeks." She smiled slightly in fond recollection. "I stayed with her until I was twenty and left for college."

She pulled back her sleeve exposing the two thick scars on her wrist. "It's odd but I'm grateful for them now. They're my reminders."

"Of what?"

She looked up into my eyes. "To live."

I thought over what she'd said. "When McKale died, I almost took my life. I had pills."

"What stopped you?"

"A voice." I felt odd saying it, but she didn't seem at all skeptical.

"What did the voice say?"

"It told me that life wasn't mine to take." I rubbed my chin. "Just before she died, McKale asked me to promise her that I would live."

She nodded. "I think we all have to make that choice. I meet dead people every day at the diner."

"What do you mean?"

"People who have given up. That's all death requires of us, to give up living."

I wondered if I was one of them.

"The thing is, the only real sign of life is growth. And growth requires pain. So to choose life is to accept pain. Some people go to such lengths to avoid pain that they give up on life. They bury their hearts, or they drug or drink themselves numb until they don't feel anything anymore. The irony is, in the end their escape becomes more painful than what they're avoiding."

I looked down for a while. "I know you're right. But I don't know if I can live without her. A part of me died with her."

"I'm so sorry," she said, rubbing my shin. After a moment she said, "You know, she's not really gone. She's still a part of you. *What* part of you is your choice. She can be a spring of gratitude and joy, or she can be a fountain of bitterness and pain. It is entirely up to you."

The thought had never occurred to me that I was making McKale into something bad.

"You have to decide to look through the pain."

"What do you mean?"

"Leah taught me that the greatest secret of life is that we find exactly what we're looking for. In spite of what happens to us, ultimately we decide whether our lives are good or bad, ugly or beautiful."

I thought this over.

"Leah told me this story. Some newspaper did an experiment. I don't remember what city it was in, but they had a man with a violin go down into the subway and play music. It was rush hour, and thousands of people passed him while he played.

"A few people threw him money, but other than that, no one paid any attention. When he finished he just walked away.

"What no one knew was that the musician was Joshua Bell, one of the greatest violinists in the world. He had just played a sold-out concert at Carnegie Hall at $100 a ticket. The piece he was playing was one of the most complex and beautiful pieces ever written, and he was playing it on a $2 million Stradivarius." She smiled at me. "I love that story," she said. "Because it sums up Leah's life. She would have stopped to listen.

"The night before I left for college Leah said to me, 'Ally, some people in this world have stopped looking for beauty, then wonder why their lives are so ugly. Don't be like them. The ability to appreciate beauty is of God. Especially in one another. Look for beauty in everyone you meet, and you'll find it. Everyone carries divinity within them. And everyone we meet has something to impart.'"

I thought of Will, the homeless man at the Jack in the Box.

"Do you still see much of Leah?" I asked.

"No. She passed away during my junior year in college." Ally's eyes welled up with tears. "She died of cancer. But I was fortunate to be with her before she passed."

She put her head down for a moment. She wiped her eyes, then looked up at me. "The night before she died I sat next to her in bed. She reached up and ran her hand across my cheek, then said to me, 'When you were brought into detention all the court could see was a troubled young lady. But I knew you were special the moment I laid eyes on you. I was right, wasn't I? Never forget, Ally, God puts people in our lives for a reason. Only through helping others can we save ourselves.' "

I nodded slowly. "That's why you asked if I was okay."

"I had this feeling that you were one of those people I was supposed to meet."

"I'm glad you did," I said.

She affectionately squeezed my foot. "I better let you get to bed."

My head was still swimming with her words. I didn't want her to go. "Do you work tomorrow?" I asked.

"No. It's my day off, and I promised a friend I'd help her paint her living room."

I stood, took her hand, and lifted her up. We walked to the door. For a moment, we just looked at each other. "Thank you," I said. "For the foot rub, the food, the food for thought . . ."

"I hope it helped." She leaned in and hugged me. When

we parted, she said, "Will you let me know when you make it to Key West?"

"Yes. How will I find you?"

"I'm on Facebook. Allyson Lynette Walker."

"Your last name is *Walker*?"

She smiled. "Yes. It should be yours."

I laughed. "I promise. I'll send you some sand."

"I'd like that." She stepped outside.

"Ally," I said.

She turned back.

"Thank you."

She leaned forward and kissed my cheek. "Have a good walk." Then she turned and walked away.

CHAPTER

Twenty-eight

We truly do not know what's in a book until it is opened.

Alan Christoffersen's diary

The next morning I just lay in bed thinking. For the first time in days, I wasn't overcome by grief. Something inside me felt different. Profoundly different. I suppose I felt hope. Or maybe I felt some part of McKale again—the *real* McKale and not the despairing phantom I'd made of her.

I got up, showered, then walked around the bungalow, gathering up things. My clothes were dry, except for two pairs of my thickest socks, which I rolled up and packed along with everything else.

I locked up the bungalow and walked over to the diner, hoping Ally might somehow be there. She wasn't. Her replacement wore a name tag that said, PEGGY SUE. I didn't ask her her real name.

I returned the key to the bungalow, then ordered a stack of banana pancakes with a 59er Scramble—a scrambled egg with ham, onion, tomato, and green pepper, topped with cheddar cheese and sour cream.

By eight-thirty, I was walking again. The road was still mostly downhill and followed the Wenatchee River, which was moving in the same direction I was walking and not much faster.

I walked all day and only stopped for a few minutes for lunch—a banana, an apple, and a couple of muffins I had bought at the diner. It was all the food I had. Peggy-Sue, the waitress, had told me there was a grocery store at Leavenworth, where I planned to stock up on supplies.

Leavenworth was exactly the way Ally had described it. The town looked as if it had been plucked from the Alps and dropped in the center of Chelan County.

The main street was lined with old-world, European street poles with decorative holiday snowflakes hanging from them. There were at least a dozen hotels and inns. I chose the one that looked the least expensive: Der Ritterhof Motor Inn.

Being in the town made me hungry for German food, and I found a suitable restaurant. I ordered a full fare: Wiener schnitzel, Leberkäse, rotkraut, and spätzle with Jäger sauce.

I remembered the one time I took McKale to a German restaurant. She was as out of place as a diabetic in a chocolate factory. She asked me if they had anything besides over-sized, fancy hot dogs. I ended up taking her to a McDonald's afterwards to get something to eat.

The memory made me laugh. I realized that it was the first time that thinking about McKale didn't make my stomach hurt. I left it up to the food to do that.

CHAPTER

Twenty-nine

I spent the night in Leavenworth—a mock Bavarian township in Washington. I had a big meal of German food, which, I suppose, will travel with me for the next fortnight. The Germans have a saying: "A good meal is worth hanging for." I'm sure this food will be hanging around for some time.

Alan Christoffersen's diary

I got up shortly after dawn. I showered and dressed, then walked across the street to the Bistro Espresso, where I ordered a light breakfast of coffee and a cheese Danish. I think I was still digesting the meal from the night before.

I finished eating, then I walked down to a bank. I put my card in the ATM and pushed the button to check my balance. There was $28,797. When I left Bellevue, there had been less than a thousand dollars in the account. Falene had been busy. *I love that woman*, I thought.

I went back to my room, packed up my things, then checked out. I walked three blocks to the Food Lion, where I stocked up on everything I needed (including a box of Hostess Ding Dongs), then hit the road.

In less than an hour, I passed through Ally's town of Peshastin. I had found myself replaying our conversation all morning. Somehow it just felt good knowing she was somewhere near.

Two hours later, I reached the town of Cashmere. There were orchards everywhere, though the trees were barren in the winter landscape. There were big fans in the fields and silver streamers tied to all the tree branches.

There was a warehouse with the Tree Top apple juice logo painted on its side. I had once tried to pitch their account. I couldn't remember why we hadn't gotten it.

Everywhere I looked there were signs for fruit—apples, apricots, cherries, and pears—and I passed by at least a dozen empty roadside fruit stands. The place was a ghost town in off-season.

At the edge of town, I sat down on a patch of straw-colored grass to stretch and eat my lunch—two foil-wrapped burritos I had bought at the Food Lion's deli.

I marveled at how completely the landscape had changed from the days before. It was now wide open and flat: a sharp contrast to the dense forests and sloping terrain that had encompassed every step of the last week. Walking on a flat road is much easier than climbing a mountain, but all things considered, I'd take the mountains. I liked the security and tranquility of the forest.

Just outside Wenatchee, I stopped and ate a simple dinner of French bread and peanut butter, which I spread with my Swiss Army pocket knife. The town center was far enough from the highway that I didn't stop. I was growing more eager to make it to Spokane. That night I slept in an apple orchard under the stars.

CHAPTER

Thirty

Long walk today, mostly orchards. The landscape has changed entirely. This land is flat, as if nature took a rolling pin to the earth.

I stopped to help a woman with car troubles.

Alan Christoffersen's diary

Rain started falling in the night, and around three in the morning, I got up and built my tent, something I was getting proficient at. When I woke at dawn, the drizzle had stopped, but the ground was wet, and by the time I was out of the orchard, my shoes were caked with several inches of mud. I did my best to kick and scrape it off, then resumed my walk.

In Orondo City, the road split, and I turned east toward Waterville and Spokane. I was in the buckle of Washington's fruit belt. More than the landscape had changed. The culture had as well. I noticed that most of the store signs were in Spanish.

I ate a sausage and egg biscuit at a gas station near the fork between Waterville and Orondo City, and I was the only one in the building who wasn't speaking Spanish.

A few miles later, the landscape grew more mountainous, and for much of the walk there was a wide gorge to my right with only a narrow walkway. The highway was dark and wet, and I was sprayed by nearly every car that passed. The road climbed again—almost as steeply as it had at the pass—and I could tell that I was much stronger than when I started my walk, as my pace barely slowed.

Two hours into the day, it began to rain again. I stopped and put on my poncho and kept walking.

On one of the tighter mountain curves, there was a car pulled over to the side next to the safety rail. Its trunk was open, and its caution lights were flashing. *Bad place to break down*, I thought. As I approached, I saw that the car, a silver-gray Malibu, was lifted up on a jack, and there were two tires lying flat on the ground, the flat tire and a spare.

I walked up to the driver's window. Inside the car was a lone woman. She was about my age or a little older, in her mid-thirties. She had blond hair that fell to her shoulders. She was holding her cell phone. A pine air freshener and a crucifix hung from her rearview mirror next to a picture of a little boy.

Her door was locked, and the window was rolled up. I rapped on her window, and it startled her. She looked up at me fearfully.

"Do you need help?" I asked.

She cracked her window a few inches.

"What?"

"Do you need any help?"

"No," she said anxiously, "my husband went to town to get help. He should be right back."

"Okay."

I'm not sure why I glanced at her left hand, but I noticed that there was no wedding ring. I considered moving on, but I was never one to leave a woman in distress, especially alone on such a dangerous stretch. I glanced back at her flat tire. "Listen, you're not safe here. It looks like you have a spare. If it's just a flat, I can change it."

She hesitated, caught between her deceit and despera-tion. Finally she said, "I lost the . . . things."

I didn't understand. "What things?"

"The metal things. The bolts."

I looked again at the wheel, then saw what she was talking about. There were no lug nuts. "What happened to them?"

"I got them off, but . . ."

She had taken them off.

". . . they rolled down the hill."

The side of the road sloped steeply down several hun-dred feet. Those babies were gone.

"How did that happen?"

"I'm just clumsy."

No lug nuts. Probably no cell phone reception. She was probably just waiting for a highway patrolman to come along, which considering where we were, could be a very long wait. "Do you mind if I put it on for you?"

She looked at me quizzically. "There's nothing to put it on with."

"We can borrow them," I said.

She was still vexed but relented. "I guess."

"Is your parking brake on?"

"Yes."

". . . and you're in park?"

"Yes."

I set down my pack. I took her tire iron and pulled a lug nut from each of the other wheels, then mounted the spare with the three nuts and tightened them. It would be enough to get her to wherever she was going. I let the car down from the jack, then put the flat tire, wrench, and jack in the trunk and slammed it down. I walked back to her window.

"You're good now. I took a nut from each of the other wheels. Just take it into a garage when you get home."

For the first time I saw her smile. "Thank you."

"Don't mention it." I lifted my pack, swinging it over one shoulder, then the other. "Have a good day."

"Wait, can I pay you?"

"No. Take care." I adjusted my hat, then walked on. The woman waited for an oncoming car to pass, then I heard the gravel spit from her tires as she pulled out onto the road. She drove slowly past me then pulled off the road fifty yards ahead where there was a small turnoff. When I reached her car, she had rolled down the window.

"Can I at least give you a ride? There's nothing on this road for miles. And it's raining. You're going to get wet."

"I'm used to getting wet," I said. "Thank you, but I'm fine. Just happy to help." I sounded as magnanimous as Superman (*Just doing my job, ma'am*), which, frankly, kind of bothered me. Einstein said, "I prefer silent vice to ostentatious virtue." I agree.

The woman looked flustered by her inability to help me. She reached into her purse and pulled out a business card and handed it to me. "Here, if you need anything, just call. That's my cell phone number."

I took the card without looking at it and slid it into my front trouser pocket. "Thanks."

"No, thank you. Have a good day."

"You too."

I waited for her to drive off in a shower of road water, then started walking again. I watched her car disappear around a bend. I wondered how long she'd been stranded there and what would have happened to her had I not come along.

The rain had stopped and the sun was high when I reached the small town of Waterville. The highway ran through the middle of town, and the local coffee shop was appropriately called *Highway 2 Brew*. I stopped for a tall coffee, a cranberry-orange muffin, and a chocolate-dipped biscotti. I sat on the concrete pad outside the coffee shop to study my map.

It looked like I would be walking through barren wilderness for the next few days—the kind of terrain you speed through in a car with your stereo turned up. I was eager to get through it.

The Waterville homes lined the highway, and it was the first time since I left Bellevue that I had walked through suburb, even a small one like this.

I thought Waterville was a peculiar name for a town that looked like Death Valley compared to what I had just walked through. At first, I guessed that the name was really just a marketing ploy like, say, Greenland—which, incidentally, is about as green as an ice cube and a whole lot colder. Then I remembered what I had learned earlier about town naming and decided that a Mr. Waterville either owned the bank or everyone's mortgages.

I wondered what people in a small town like this did for entertainment until I saw Randy's Ice Cream Parlor and

Putt Putt Golf Course. I'm betting that the average citizen of Waterville could putt like Jack Nicklaus.

After another twenty miles, I reached Douglas. There were no services on the road, so I walked a hundred or so yards off the highway and pitched my tent. It was cold as the sunset, just a little above freezing. I wanted to make a fire, but there was nothing to burn.

For the first time on my journey, I took out my portable stove and fired it up. I opened the can of SpaghettiOs I had purchased in Leavenworth, tore off its wrapper, then set the can on the blue propane flame until it started to boil. Unfortunately, I had forgotten to buy utensils. I tore off a piece of French bread and used it to scoop up the spaghetti. For dessert I ate a Ding Dong. I rolled its foil wrapping into a ball and threw it at a rabbit that was watching from the outskirts of my camp. I missed.

For the first time that week, the stars were visible. For me, it was one of those times we all have when we look up at the night sky and feel remarkably insignificant. That was a hopeful thing. Maybe God had more on His plate than ruining my life. I climbed inside my tent and went to sleep.

CHAPTER

Thirty-one

The time has come, the walker said, to talk of many things. Of crop circles and UFOs and the tourists these things bring . . .

(My apologies to Lewis Carroll)

Alan Christoffersen's diary

The next few days of travel were tedious and largely forgettable. I walked from Douglas to Coulee, Coulee to Wilbur and Wilbur to Davenport, averaging about 28 miles a day.

Fortunately there were places along the way to stay and eat. In Coulee, I lodged at the Ala Cozy Motel and had a green chili burrito next door at Big Wally's Shell Station and Bait and Tackle Shop. I only wished they sold T-shirts.

Coulee had an industrial feel, and it made me miss walking in the mountains even more. I realized how fortunate I'd been that the first part of my walk had led me through nature and her healing. In this landscape, there was nothing to do but walk and think.

It was a 30-mile walk to Wilbur—the biggest city I'd been through in days. Wilbur was a proper city with a bank, a real estate office, and a medical clinic. I stopped at the Eight Bar B Hotel, which claimed the "largest rooms in the county," which seemed a reasonable claim. The hotel was located next to a small burger joint called the Billy Burger.

I left my pack in the room, then went to the Billy Burger to get something to eat. I was famished, and I ordered the Wild Goose Bill Burger named after the founder of Wilbur, Wild Goose Bill. I was sure there was a story there, but I never got around to asking.

The Billy Burger's walls were lined with the largest (and only) salt-and-pepper-shaker collection I had ever seen, which included a pair of dice with Vegas written in gold glitter, a couple of hula girls, some politically incorrect Little Black Sambo shakers, a washer and dryer, and a seated JFK.

They also sold Billy Burger T-shirts and a book chronicling the history of Wilbur, which I seriously doubt will ever hit the *New York Times* bestseller list, though stranger things have happened. I had noticed that nearly everything in Wilbur started with the letter B, and I asked the woman at the counter, Kate, why.

"Good question," she said. "A big shot Wilbur citizen, Benjamin B. Banks, had eight sons, and he and the missus, Belva, gave 'em all names startin' with B.

"He was big on hard work, so he made all his kids start businesses to fund their college tuitions. Billy Burger was Billy's project. He sold it when he left for school."

That explained the Eight Bar B Hotel as well. As I was eating, I noticed a plaque on the wall.

Certificate of Award
Thanks to the Aliens who made
Wilbur their Vacation Destination.

Beneath the plaque was a framed, double-spread newspaper page with pictures of crop circles. I had seen these pictures somewhere before, but I didn't know they had come from Washington. I got up to read the article.

Apparently the little town of Wilbur had been blessed with crop circles not once, but twice. The first was discovered by a crop duster in the spring of 2007. The second appeared two years later, in 2009.

I said to Kate, "This happened here?"

"You betcha. Twice. Over at Jesse Beales' place."

"What is it," I asked, "local teens playing a prank?"

The woman's eyebrows fell. "No sir. Ain't no one here done them. They came from the sky. There weren't no tracks in nor out of the field. The trails you see on that picture there were caused by the tourists and UFO chasers."

"Tourists come to see these?"

"Yes, sir. From all over the world. Really put Wilbur on the map. They come wearin' football helmets wrapped in tinfoil and Jesus robes. Mr. Beales says those aliens owe him $500, and he's gonna get it, even if he has to take it from their sorry green hides."

"That would be some headline," I mused. "Farmer assaults aliens with pitchfork. World destroyed."

The woman didn't smile.

"Mr. Beales should just charge the tourists admission," I said.

She looked at me as if I'd just solved world hunger. "That's a darn good idea. I'll mention that next time he comes by."

"So you think the crop circles were made by aliens?"

"No, sir."

I turned to face her. "But you said they came from the sky."

"Air Force," she said, her voice dropping as if to avoid detection. "They done it."

"The Air Force did it?"

"Yes sir. We got Fairchild Air Force Base just down the road a piece. They're always conducting top-secret research. Probably some new, high-tech laser beam."

I thought of another headline but kept it to myself. *Air Force declares war on Farmer Beales, burns circles in crops.*

"Course it could also just be aliens," she relented. "It's a strange world we live in. You never know."

"No," I agreed, "you never know." I sat back down and finished eating. "That was a good burger. Thank you."

"We got shakes too. Intergalactically famous."

CHAPTER

Thirty-two

It is good to walk. Even if you have somewhere to go.

Alan Christoffersen's diary

I was tempted to stop and see the crop circles but not curious enough to add the miles.

Eight miles out of Wilbur, I stopped for breakfast at a roadside café in a tiny farming town called Creston, which, incidentally, I thought was a much better town name for an alien landing.

I ordered biscuits, fried ham, and scrambled eggs, which I heavily seasoned with Tabasco sauce. The café's chef and proprietor (he introduced himself as Mr. Saville), was a balding Korean War veteran with a Marines tattoo and the build of a greasy-spoon chef.

It was as if Mr. Saville hadn't talked to anyone for a few years as he spoke nonstop about whatever came to mind, though most of what came to his mind involved the New World Order conspiracy and 1992 Populist presidential candidate and former Delta Force commander "Bo" Gritz.

Mr. Saville was a life-long resident of Creston and was proud to inform me that Harry Tracy, the final surviving member of the Hole in the Wall Gang, was shot at a Creston ranch not 3 miles from the café. I suppose every city has its claim to fame.

I paid my bill, promised I'd buy Mr. Gritz's book, and started off again. It was a long, dull day of walking, and the afternoon's highlight was watching a bobcat cross the highway about 50 yards ahead of me. I wasn't sure if I should be worried about the animal or not. I'd read that bobcats rarely attack humans and usually only when they're rabid, which really isn't a comforting thought since, if I had my druthers, I'd rather be attacked by a non-rabid bobcat. Just in case, I picked up a large rock from the side of the road, which turned out to be a total waste of motion since the cat was gone when I stood back up.

It was twilight when I reached the town of Davenport—a real town with a Lion's Club sign at its entrance. It also had a pretty good Mexican restaurant where I ordered the chile verde burrito combo plate and a flan dessert. McKale always ordered the flan dessert.

As I was paying my bill, I asked the waitress where I should spend the night. The way she looked at me made me a little uncomfortable, and I was afraid that she was going to suggest her place. I was relieved when she suggested the Morgan Street Bed and Breakfast and Coffee Shop just a few blocks further down the highway. I left her a $5 tip, lifted my pack, and walked off to find the inn.

CHAPTER

Thirty-three

The proprietor at the Bed and Breakfast
had been through Bali, China, Nepal,
Europe, and death. But not in that order.

Alan Christoffersen's diary

The Morgan Street Bed and Breakfast was a quaint, Victorian-style home built in 1896. It was simple, as far as Victorian motifs go, though it still had some decorative spindling, a large, front-facing gable, and a Queen Anne turret with a bell-shaped dome.

McKale would have loved this place, I thought. McKale was a bed-and-breakfast connoisseur. As I wrote before, her surprise plan for our lost weekend was to stay in a bed and breakfast on Orcas Island. She had made a list of B&Bs in the Pacific Northwest, and every few months we'd hit one of them. One time, when I was too busy with work, she stayed in one on her own.

I pushed open the wrought-iron gate and walked up to the porch. The front door was locked, so I rang the door-bell and almost immediately heard footsteps. A deadbolt slid, and the door opened to a middle-aged woman with silver hair and blue-rimmed glasses. She wore a yellow sweater over a red print dress.

"May I help you?"

"Hi. Do you have any vacancies?"

She smiled. "Yes, we do. Come right in." She stepped back from the door.

I walked inside onto a Persian rug. The room was warm and elegant.

"Just set your pack down right there," she said, pointing to the floor next to the stairwell.

"Thank you."

She walked over to a mahogany Victorian writing desk against the wall and pulled a register from a cubby. "Are you alone?"

"Yes, ma'am." I slid the pack from my shoulder and leaned it against the wall.

"Your name, please."

"Alan Christoffersen."

She looked up. "Are you related to that singer?"

"No. It's not spelled the same."

She went back to her register. "Very well. We've only one other guest tonight, so you have your choice of rooms. They're all nice, unless you have an aversion to stairs."

"I'm fine with stairs."

"They're all the same price, too, except the honeymoon suite. I don't suppose you'll be wanting that."

"No, ma'am."

"My name is Colleen Hammersmith. But you may call me Colleen."

"Thank you."

"I'll put you in the green room. It has a nice new mattress and duvet I picked out myself. I'll just need your credit card and some ID."

I took out my wallet and pulled out the essentials. "There you go."

She swiped my credit card, then handed me back my

card and license with a slip of paper and pen. "Please just sign there."

I signed the form.

"And here's your key." She handed me a brass skeleton key. "You're in room C, right at the top of the stairway. The bathroom is at the end of the hallway. It's shared with the other room, but you're the only one on the second floor tonight. My room is just down this hallway, to the left next to the kitchen. Please let me know if you need anything."

"Thank you. I'm sure I'll be fine." I retrieved my pack and carried it up the stairs. I unlocked the door, then stepped inside. The space was dimly lit by a brass floor lamp, and I turned on the overhead light.

The room was tidy and feminine, decorated in typical Victorian style with cream walls adorned with framed pictures of flowers—lilies and daffodils—a gold-framed mirror, and shadow boxes displaying antique toys. There was a tall, antique French-style armoire and a small, leather-topped round table with ball-and-claw feet. In the center of the room, there was a large bed with a solid mahogany headboard and a floral-patterned duvet piled high with lace-trimmed shams.

I took off my pack and laid it against the wall, then removed my parka and set it on top of my pack. I walked to the window and parted the curtains. The only view was of the Strate Funeral Home and parking lot across the street. I pulled down the blind, then undressed, laying my clothes and shoes at the foot of the bed. I pulled the duvet down to the foot of the bed, piled the shams in a corner of the room, then peeled back the sheets and lay back on the bed. The sheets smelled fresh, the way they did when McKale pulled them out of the dryer. In fact, the whole room smelled good, like lavender, and I noticed a purple fabric sachet on the nightstand next to me. The experience was a far cry from the shack I'd camped in only earlier in the week. As I lay there thinking, there was a knock on the door. Actually, more of a kick.

"Just a minute," I said. I got up and put on the robe that hung from the closet door, then opened the door. Mrs. Hammersmith stood there balancing a basket of blue-berry scones in the crook of one arm and holding a saucer and a teacup filled with steaming water and a small wicker basket filled with tea and sweeteners.

"I thought you might like some tea before you went to bed."

"Thank you."

She stepped past me, setting everything down on the nightstand. "There's a spoon in the service." She smiled at me. "Nothing like a spot of hot tea to help you sleep well." She walked back to the door. "I won't bother you anymore. Good night."

"Night." I began to shut the door.

"Mr. Christoffersen, I forgot to ask, what time do you think you'll be wanting breakfast?"

"Maybe seven, seven thirty."

"I'm an early riser so I'll have the crossword done by then. I'll be making my raspberry muffins and egg frittata. Do you eat ham?"

"Yes."

"Frittata with cheddar and ham it is." She turned and walked down the stairs. I shut the door and locked it, then turned off the light, leaving the room lit only by the floor lamp.

I sat down on the bed and dropped a bag of tea into the cup. As it steeped, I took a bite of the scone. It tasted good, but I was still full from dinner, so I put it back in its basket. I lifted the tea bag out of the cup and lay it on the saucer, then poured in two packages of Sweet 'n Low. I stirred it with the spoon, then lay it, with the saucer, next to the bed. I slowly sipped the tea.

The room was comfortable and warm, but I wasn't happy there. The surroundings were too similar to what McKale and I had experienced together. It was like going to a party where the hostess was missing.

My heart ached and I began fearing the onset of another panic attack. I set down my tea, turned out the lights, and climbed under the covers, hoping to fall asleep before panic found me.

I woke around seven or so, the morning sun leaking through the sides of the drawn blind. I put on my robe, grabbed some fresh clothes and underwear, then walked down the hall to the bathroom and showered and shaved. Walking back to my room, I could hear the clinking of dinnerware downstairs in the dining room. The delicious smell of home cooking wafted upstairs.

I hung up the robe, pulled my road atlas from my bag, and walked downstairs. To my surprise there were no other guests in the dining room. Mrs. Hammersmith smiled when she saw me.

"Good morning, Mr. Christoffersen," she said brightly.

"Call me Alan," I said.

"Alan it is," she replied. "I have a nephew named Alan. He's quite an accomplished cellist."

"Then a name is all we share," I said. "My musical ability is pretty much confined to my iPod."

She smiled. "I hope you're hungry. I've always had trouble cooking for so few people. I always make too much food."

"I'm famished. Where would you like me to sit?"

"Wherever you like. This table by the window is nice."

I walked over to it and sat down. "Am I the only guest here?"

"You are now. The Gandleys left just a few minutes before you came down. Gigi was eager to get home to Boise. Would you like some coffee?"

"Yes, please."

She walked over to a service table to get the coffee pot. "Did you sleep well? Was the bed okay?"

I hadn't slept well, but the bed had nothing to do with it. "The bed was great. Very soft."

"Not too soft, I hope. It's a new mattress. How was the room?"

"The room is beautiful. My wife . . ." I stopped myself.

"Your wife?"

"Nothing," I said.

She looked at me for a moment, then began pouring the coffee. "I'm pleased to hear you liked the room. I must tell you, one or two people have complained about the view of the funeral home. Personally, I just think they were afraid of death."

"Well, I can understand that. Everyone fears death."

She stopped pouring and set the pot down on a nearby table. "I don't," she said. "At least not since I was twelve."

I looked at her curiously. "Why twelve?"

"Because that's when I died," she said. "I'll be right back with your breakfast."

She walked out of the dining room, leaving me to mull over the statement she'd dropped so casually, as if it hadn't required explanation. She returned about three minutes later, carrying a plate. "Here's your ham-and-cheese frittata. And this is a raspberry crumb muffin. You're going to love it. I got the recipe from Magnolia Bakery in New York City. It's out of this world."

She set the plate in front of me. I had less interest in the food than what she'd said. "What did you mean about dying when you were twelve?"

"Just that I died."

I wondered what I was missing. "But you're not dead."

"No. I came back."

"Back from death?"

She nodded.

I had always been fascinated by stories of near-death experiences. "Would you tell me about it?"

She looked at me for a moment then said, "I don't think

so. People get a little . . . ," she carefully chose a word, ". . . *upset* about it."

"Please. It would mean a lot to me."

She looked at me for a moment, then sighed. "Okay. You eat, I'll talk."

She sat in the chair across from me. "The summer I was twelve, my little brother and I climbed a tree in our front yard. We hadn't noticed that the tree had grown over some power lines, and as I was climbing, I accidentally grabbed a power line. All I remember was a flash of light and a loud snap. Seven thousand volts went through my body. It actually blew holes through the bottoms of my Keds. It melted the flesh where I grabbed it." She held up her hand. "It left me with this." There was a deep, channel-like scar crossing her fingers. She looked at me. "You're not eating."

"Sorry." I took an obligatory bite.

"I fell about twelve feet to the ground. My brother climbed down the tree and ran to the house, screaming for my mother. I knew this because I followed him into the house. I didn't realize what was happening until the door slammed in front of me, and I went right through it."

I looked at her quizzically. "You mean your ghost?"

"My spirit," she said, as if the word *ghost* bothered her. "My mother came running out, and we all ran to see my body. I tell you, it's a peculiar thing looking down at yourself. You don't think of it, but our perception of ourselves is what we see from pictures or the mirror—always two dimensional. I realized that I had never really seen myself before. Not the way others see me. I looked different than I thought I did.

"My mother started shaking my body, and there I was, standing next to her, watching her do it. I said, 'I'm over here, Mom.' But she couldn't hear me. She just put her ear to my chest.

"Suddenly there was a light in front of me. You hear people talk about *the light*. They say, go toward the light. I don't think I went toward the light. I think it came to me. It was right there, passing through me.

"Suddenly I was somewhere else, and there was a being of light standing next to me. I had this feeling of perfect joy, like all the best moments of my life, all the Christmas mornings and summer vacations and new loves, everything all rolled up together but more. The feeling was indescribable.

"The Being told me that I wasn't supposed to be there yet and that I needed to go back to earth. I remember that I didn't want to go. I begged Him to let me stay with Him. But He said I would be gone just a short time, then I could come back after I had finished my mission.

"Then I was suddenly back in my body. I was lying on the ground, and I started crying from the pain. My mother told me that night that she couldn't hear my heart beating, and she thought I was dead. It was several years later that I told her what had happened to me."

"Did she believe you?"

"Yes. She always believed me. I never gave her reason to doubt."

"What did she think?"

"I'm not sure what she thought, but she said she was glad they made me come back."

"What was that you said earlier about your mission?"

"Everyone has a purpose for coming to earth. I hadn't finished mine."

"So what is your mission?"

"Nothing that will make headlines, if that's what you're wondering. Actually, I've spent my life trying to figure that out. It took me years to realize that the searching *was* the path. It was simple. My mission is to live. And accept what comes my way until I get to go back home. My *real* home."

"You sound eager to get back."

"I suppose I am. I'm not crazy about what I'm going to have to go through to get there, but I tell you, it's worth the trip. Kind of like a trip to Bali."

"You've been to Bali?" I asked.

"Bali, Nepal, Italy, China, Taiwan. Just because I live in Davenport doesn't mean I haven't seen the world."

"You're fortunate to have had that experience."

"People have said that, but I don't know. It has made my life harder. I've always felt different, like I don't belong here. But, I suppose, that's the point. None of us belong here."

"As I grew older, I had a lot of questions. I talked to a psychiatrist, but he thought I was crazy and gave me a prescription for Prozac. I told a priest, and he told me not to talk about it. I never understood that. When I was nineteen, I learned that there are groups of people who have had experiences like mine. So I went to one of their conferences. It validated what I'd experienced, but the people weren't real happy. People who have had NDEs, that's what they called them, have trouble keeping jobs or staying married. I guess we just get bored with what's here. Normal people don't know anything else, so they live as if this life is everything.

"It's like Mrs. Santos, down the road at the Delgado ranch. The farthest away she's ever been from home is Seattle. She has no idea what's out there. She can't even comprehend the mist rising off Sun Moon lake or the way the Italian sun gilds the Chianti vineyards. In a way that's the way the Life-huggers are."

"Life-huggers?"

"I made that word up. They're people who hang on to this life because they think this is it. But they're fools, thinking they can hold on to this life. Everything in this world passes. Everything. You can't hold on to a single thing. But God knows they try. Some people even freeze their bodies so they can be woken again at some future time. Fools. All they have to do is look around and they can see that nothing here lasts."

"Well, not all of us have the benefit of seeing the other side," I said somewhat defensively.

"No, but there's evidence of the other side everywhere. Just ask anyone who works with death—like geriatric doctors and hospice workers. Any of them will tell you what happens when someone dies. How often it is that someone dying looks up and greets a visitor from that other side. It's the rule, not the exception. But no one ever talks about that. They don't even talk about death, as if not talking about it will make it go away. How can you understand life if you don't understand death?" She looked down at my plate. "Now you haven't been eating. Everything's cold. Let me go warm that up for you."

She lifted my plate and carried it back to the kitchen. Ironically, what she had said about the Life-huggers was the same thought I'd had about the inhabitants of the little towns I'd walked through, wondering if they knew that there's a whole world out there. But the truth was, I was no different than them. I was a Life-hugger.

Mrs. Hammersmith came back a few minutes later, carrying my plate with an oven mitt. "Be careful. The plate's a little hot." She set the plate in front of me.

"Thank you." I lifted a fork. "And thank you for sharing your story."

"You just keep one thing in mind, Alan. Death is the beginning. This is Winter. Spring is what comes next." She sighed. "I'd better get back to work. Owning a B&B is like having a large family. Someone always needs something."

With that she walked out. I finished eating my breakfast, then went back upstairs. I took out my map and looked it over, then collected my things and walked back downstairs. Mrs. Hammersmith was clearing my table.

"You're off?" she said.

"Back to the road. Could you tell me how many miles we are from Spokane?"

"We're a little ways. About 36 miles, give or take a few." She smiled. "I hope you enjoyed your stay."

"Very much so." I walked to the door. "Thanks again for everything. You've given me a lot to think about."

"You're welcome," she said warmly. "Oh, just a minute." She ran back to the kitchen, then returned, carrying a muffin wrapped in a napkin. "One for the road. Come back and visit us again."

"I might just do that." I walked out grateful for my stay.

As I walked out of Davenport, I wondered if I could really make it to Spokane by nightfall. The farthest I had walked in a single day was 31 miles, and I was pretty exhausted at that. Still, I felt good and I was eager to reach my first destination. I decided just to see what the day had in store.

Without food supplies, I was carrying less in my pack, and I made good time. I stopped for lunch at Dean's Drive-in. They, too, had world-famous shakes, though they limited their claim to their huckleberry shakes. I entered Spokane County at two in the afternoon, and three hours later, I reached the west end of Fairchild Air Force Base. The base was situated on an enormous piece of land and was a city unto itself. I wondered why they didn't just burn crop circles on their own property.

At eight o'clock I stopped at the Hong Kong Restaurant and Bar for dinner in the town of Airway Heights. I still hadn't completely made up my mind whether or not to press on to Spokane, but I was still feeling good, so after eating a meal of kung pao shrimp and potstickers, I just kept walking.

I felt optimistic about my odds of making it to Spokane until about eleven o'clock, when my body hit some invisible physical wall, perhaps the same one marathon runners talk about. Suddenly I was just too exhausted to go any farther.

I forced myself on until I saw a hotel in the distance. I practically limped into the Hilton Garden Inn next to the Rusty Moose Restaurant. Surprisingly, the hotel had no vacancies. The man behind the counter casually suggested that I just drive on a few more miles to Spokane.

I thought about resting my legs in the hotel's warm lobby but decided against it, afraid that if I stopped to rest, my legs might cramp up—another casual decision I would live to regret. I thanked the clerk and walked back out to the highway, promising myself that I would take the next day off. It was a promise I would keep, though not for any reason I had considered.

CHAPTER

Thirty-four

It seems as if the golden rule has changed to "do unto others what it takes to get their gold."

Alan Christoffersen's diary

The temperature had dropped below fifty, and my legs were heavy, as if they had weights attached. I had walked more than 35 miles, and I was practically asleep on my feet.

It was past midnight when the headlamps of a car flashed behind me. As the car neared, I could hear it slowing down. I thought they might be stopping to ask directions, or, God willing, to offer me a ride, so I turned back.

The car was an older model, a pimped four-door Impala, yellow with a black racing stripe. I could hear its music before it reached me, the heavy pounding base of rap. The car pulled up to my side and slowed to my gait. An ugly kid with pocked skin leaned out the window.

"Hey, what's up?"

I noticed the car was full of kids. "Nothing," I said. "Just walking."

"Whatcha got there?"

"Nothing." I kept walking, hoping the guys would lose interest. Another car drove by. The kid said something to the driver, and the car's tires squealed as it fishtailed off the road in front of me. The doors flew open, and five youths climbed out. Unfortunately, the kid in the window was the smallest of the group. One of the guys was a monster, at least six inches taller than me. His arms were folded at his chest, and he had tattoos and scars up both arms.

The gang surrounded me.

"What you got on your back?" ugly kid said.

"Nothing you'd want."

"Give it to me."

"You don't want to do this," I said.

He scowled. "You don't tell me what I want, man."

"We're gonna mess you up," someone said behind me.

My eyes darted back and forth between them. I changed my mind. "You can have my pack," I said.

"We'll take that after we're done," a new voice said.

"We were lookin' to roll some bums," ugly kid said. "And here you are."

"This isn't cool," I said. "Why don't you just get back in your car . . ."

Ugly kid said to the monster, "He talkin' again. You should shut him up."

The circle closed in.

I took off my pack. "Hey, come on, why are you . . ."

I never finished. The first hit landed on the back of my head. It wasn't a fist. Something wood, like a club. I saw a flash of light but somehow kept on my feet. As I grabbed my head, two of them came at me, ugly kid and one other.

I swung wildly at ugly kid and caught him hard enough to knock him down. One of his friends laughed at him, and I heard him shout out an obscenity as he climbed back to his feet. He came back at me.

The next few minutes seemed to pass in slow motion, like a nightmare when you want to run, but you can't move. I was knocked to the ground, then was hit and kicked from all sides. I had my arms up, trying to protect my face, while the monster kept stomping on my head with boots that felt like they weighed a hundred pounds.

Suddenly the attack stopped. I rolled over to my side, coughing up fluid. There was blood dripping down my face. Ugly kid held a knife.

"You wanna die, loser?"

I looked at him standing above me, my vision blurred from the assault. There was my chance. This thug could finish what I wasn't willing or able to do. Life or death. Somehow I felt it was really my choice.

"No," I said, "I don't."

"Ain't your choice," he said.

Just then a boot landed squarely in my face, knocking me out.

CHAPTER

Thirty-five

Kierkegaard wrote that "we understand our lives backward, but must live them forward." He was right, of course; but in looking back on the hammer strikes that chisel and shape our souls we understand more than our lives and even ourselves— we begin to comprehend the sculptor.

Alan Christoffersen's diary

I would describe what I experienced next as an out-of-body experience except there was too much pain. Excruciating pain.

Someone was kneeling next to me. Around me I heard voices, different voices than my assailants. Older. Cleaner. They swirled around me, speaking about me, over me, none of them to me—as if I weren't there. I suppose, on some level that was true.

I couldn't speak. I couldn't even grunt to acknowledge that I heard them. My eyes were closed or mostly closed, and I could not really see people, just blurs of moving colors against the occasional flash of passing cars and a streetlight glaring above me, though it might have been the moon. The lights still hurt my eyes. There were also flashing lights of red and blue.

I began to differentiate the voices. I heard an angry, older voice shout, "Stay on the ground!" I assumed the command wasn't for me.

Then someone pressed against me and pain filled my entire body. A dark blur said something I didn't understand. Then there were two lighter blurs, and the dark figure disappeared. The pressure on my side increased. I could feel something wet run down my stomach.

Someone pulled my shirt up. The fabric stuck to my

side, and I could feel something pull away from my skin, like a bandage.

My left side below my ribcage throbbed with pain. The right side of my head pounded. My hair was wet. *Why was my hair wet?*

Someone grabbed my wrist; a finger prodded for my pulse. A cuff was placed around my arm.

I heard the crisp static crackle of a radio.

The dialogue was closer, clearer. "Pulse is steady. Blood pressure is low, sixty over twenty. He's lost a lot of blood. Call ahead to Sacred Heart."

"Better call his next of kin. Any ID?"

"You checked all his pockets?"

I felt a hand move down my right leg. Then my left.

"Here's something."

I was lifted from the ground, and I felt a plastic mask being fitted over my nose and mouth. Just then a phrase came to mind from my former life. My ad-guy life. *Fade to black.*

CHAPTER

Thirty-six

Death is not the end.

Alan Christoffersen's diary

I wrote in the beginning of this book that there are things that happened to me that you might not believe. This is one of the times I was writing about. So feel free to skip over this part. Or not. Just don't say I didn't warn you.

To this day, I can't say for sure what happened at that moment. So I'll just put it down as I perceived it and let you draw your own conclusions—which I'm sure you'll do anyway. It's a rare human who spends more time looking for truth than protecting their already-held beliefs.

Somewhere in the murky, gray twilight between consciousness and sleep, McKale came to me. Call it a dream or delirium, if that makes you feel safe, but she was there. I saw her. I heard her. I felt her.

The Bard wrote, *"There are more things in heaven and earth . . . than are dreamt of in your philosophy . . ."* That's especially true today, in our age of unbelief. Frankly, it doesn't matter to me if you don't believe that this really happened, just so long as you believe that I do.

Somehow McKale was kneeling next to me. Not on the ground. We weren't on ground. I don't know where we were. Someplace soft and white. She looked impossibly beautiful; her skin was fresh and translucent, as if it glowed from its own light. Perfect. She smiled at me with joyful radiance. And when she spoke, her voice was sweet, like the ring of crystal. "Hello, my love."

"McKale." I tried to sit up but was unable to move. "Did they kill me?" I felt hopeful asking this.

"No."

I stared at her. "Are you real?"

She smiled. "Of course."

"Is this a dream?"

She didn't answer.

"Where have you been?"

"Near. Very near. Death is like being in the next room."

"Will we be together again?"

She smiled, and I knew the answer before she spoke. But it didn't come from her. It was as if I somehow remembered it.

"Of course. But not now. You're not finished. There are still people who need you. And people you need."

"I only needed you."

Her words were loving but firm. "That was never true. You were meant for more than just me."

"What people? Who will come?"

"Many. Angel."

"Angel? An angel?" I asked. "What do you mean?"

She leaned over and kissed me, and it was the sweetest thing I'd ever felt. "Don't worry, my love. Your path is seeking you. She'll find you."

Then she was gone.

CHAPTER

Thirty-seven

I do not know what lies beyond the horizon, only that the road I walk was meant for me. It is enough.

Alan Christoffersen's diary

I awoke in a soft bed, swaddled in clean, white sheets. A plastic tube circled my ears and was blowing oxygen into my nose. There were metal bars at my sides. Something was constricting me. I reached down. There were bandages across my abdomen.

I was suddenly aware that a woman was sitting next to me. I turned to look at her. My vision was still a little blurred, and there was a window behind her, making it look as if she were glowing. I didn't know who she was, though something about her looked familiar. I didn't even know where I was.

"Welcome back," she said softly.

For a moment, I just looked at her. My mouth was dry, and my tongue stuck to my mouth as I tried to speak. "Where am I?"

"Sacred Heart Hospital in Spokane."

"Who are you?"

"I'm the woman you stopped to help outside of Waterville."

I didn't understand. "Waterville?"

"Remember? You fixed my tire?"

I remembered. It already seemed like a long time ago. "I should have taken you up on the ride."

She smiled wryly. "I think so."

Her being there made no sense to me. Nothing at that moment made sense to me. "Why are you here?"

"The police called me. They found the card I gave you. They said it was the only phone number they could find on you." She reached over and touched my arm. "How do you feel?"

"Everything hurts." As if in consequence of my words there was a sudden shock of pain that took my breath. I groaned.

"Careful," she said.

"What happened to me?"

"A gang jumped you. They beat you up pretty bad."

"I thought they were going to kill me."

"They might have if it wasn't for the two men driving by. They were coming back from hunting and had shot-guns. They probably saved your life."

I closed my eyes.

"I have the men's phone numbers. In case you want to thank them."

"Did they take my pack?"

"A police officer told me they have your things."

A few minutes later, a doctor walked in. She was young and looked a little like Monnie, my former neighbor, though her hair was red and short. She inspected my I.V., then looked up at me. "How are you feeling?"

"I'm not dead yet."

She grinned. "That's what I was hoping. I'm Doctor Tripp. You had a close call. You lost a lot of blood."

"How long have I been here?"

"You came in around one A.M. and . . . ," she checked her watch, "it's almost two."

My head was foggy. "Two in the morning?"

"In the afternoon," she said.

"What happened to my stomach?"

"You were stabbed. You had to be given a blood transfusion."

"How many times was I stabbed?"

"You have two major wounds to your belly and one flesh wound in your side. Luckily they missed your liver, or you'd be in much worse shape. You also have a concussion."

"That's why my head hurts," I said. "The big guy kept stomping on my head."

"They worked you over pretty good. You really need to find a different set of friends to hang out with."

"I'll remember that."

"The police would like to talk to you when you feel up to it. They're just down the hall."

"They're here?"

"One of the young men who attacked you was shot. He's in ICU." She added, "Don't worry, he's not going anywhere. Except jail." She turned to the woman next to me. "Are you his wife?"

"I'm a friend."

I exhaled slowly. "How long will I be here?" I asked.

"A while. At least a few days. Maybe a week."

"I need to get back out walking."

Her brow furrowed. "Sorry, but you'll have to put your

plans on hold. You're in no condition to walk. Your next stop is home."

I didn't respond.

"Where is home?" the woman asked.

"I'm homeless," I said. I felt awkward saying it out loud.

"He can come home with me," the woman said.

The doctor nodded. "Okay, we'll deal with that when we get there. I'll be back in a few hours to check up on you." She touched my shoulder. "I'm glad to see you're doing so well." She walked out of the room.

I turned to the woman. "You don't even know me."

"I know you're the kind of guy who stops to help a stranger. Besides, you didn't know me when you came to my rescue. I'm just returning the favor."

"How do you know I'm not a serial killer?"

"If you were, you wouldn't have turned down the ride when I offered it to you."

She had a point. "Probably not," I said. I lay back and took a deep breath. This wasn't a detour I had planned on. Of course, that pretty much summed up my life. "I don't even know your name," I said.

"Sorry." She reached out and touched my hand. "It's Annie. But everyone calls me Angel."

EPILOGUE

When I was a boy, my second-grade schoolteacher read us a Brazilian folk tale called *The Little Cow*.

A Master of Wisdom was walking through the countryside with his apprentice when they came to a small, disheveled hovel on a meager piece of farmland. "See this poor family," said the Master. "Go see if they will share with us their food."

"But we have plenty," said the apprentice.

"Do as I say."

The obedient apprentice went to the home. The good farmer and his wife, surrounded by their seven children, came to the door. Their clothes were dirty and in tatters.

"Fair greetings," said the apprentice. "My Master and I are sojourners and want for food. I've come to see if you have any to share."

The farmer said, "We have little, but what we have we will share." He walked away, then returned with a small piece of cheese and a crust of bread. "I am sorry, but we don't have much."

The apprentice did not want to take their food but did as he had been instructed. "Thank you. Your sacrifice is great."

"Life is difficult," the farmer said, "but we get by. And in spite of our poverty, we do have one great blessing."

"What blessing is that?" asked the apprentice.

"We have a little cow. She provides us milk and cheese, which we eat or sell in the marketplace. It is not much but she provides enough for us to live on."

The apprentice went back to his Master with the meager rations and reported what he had learned about the farmer's plight. The Master of Wisdom said, "I am pleased to hear of their generosity, but I am greatly sorrowed by their circumstance. Before we leave this place, I have one more task for you."

"Speak, Master."

"Return to the hovel and bring back their cow."

The apprentice did not know why, but he knew his Master to be merciful and wise, so he did as he was told. When he returned with the cow, he said to his Master, "I have done as you commanded. Now what is it that you would do with this cow?"

"See yonder cliffs? Take the cow to the highest crest and push her over."

The apprentice was stunned. "But Master . . ."

"Do as I say."

The apprentice sorrowfully obeyed. When he had completed his task, the Master and his apprentice went on their way.

Over the next years, the apprentice grew in mercy and wisdom. But every time he thought back on the visit to the poor farmer's family, he felt a pang of guilt. One day he decided to go back to the farmer and apologize for what he had done. But when he arrived at the farm, the small hovel was gone. Instead there was a large, fenced villa.

"Oh, no," he cried. "The poor family who was here was driven out by my evil deed." Determined to learn what had become of the family, he went to the villa and pounded on its great door. The door was answered by a servant. "I would like to speak to the master of the house," he said.

"As you wish," said the servant. A moment later the apprentice was greeted by a smiling, well-dressed man.

"How may I serve you?" the wealthy man asked.

"Pardon me, sir, but could you tell me what has become of the family who once lived on this land but is no more?"

"I do not know what you speak of," the man replied. "My family has lived on this land for three generations."

The apprentice looked at him quizzically. "Many years ago I walked through this valley, where I met a farmer and his seven children. But they were very poor and lived in a small hovel."

"Oh," the man said smiling, "that was my family. But my children have all grown now and have their own estates."

The apprentice was astonished. "But you are no longer poor. What happened?"

"God works in mysterious ways," the man said, smiling. "We had this little cow who provided us with the slimmest of necessities, enough to survive but little more. We suffered but expected no more from life. Then, one day, our little cow wandered off and fell over a cliff. We knew that we would be ruined without her, so we did everything we could to survive. Only then did we discover that we had greater power and abilities than we possibly imagined and never would have found as long as we relied on that cow. What a great blessing from Heaven to have lost our little cow."

This is what I've learned. We can spend our days bemoaning our losses, or we can grow from them. Ultimately the choice is ours. We can be victims of circumstance or masters of our own fate, but make no mistake, *we cannot be both*.

We are all on a walk. Perhaps not as literal as mine, but a walk all the same. I don't know what lies ahead of me, but I have 3,000 miles to find out. There are people I've yet to meet who are waiting for my path to intersect with theirs, so they can complete their own journeys. I don't know who or where they are, but I know for certain that they are waiting.

You don't know me. I am no one famous or important. But, like you, I arrived here with a round-trip ticket. Someday I'll go back to that place from whence I came. Back home where McKale waits.

When that time comes, I'll look her in the eyes and tell her I kept the promise—that I chose to live. She'll smile and laugh then say, "I can't believe you walked across the entire continent, you crazy old coot."

That's the way I imagine it will be. I could be wrong, but I don't think so. Sometimes, in the shadowlands of my dreams, she whispers to me that she's waiting. And in those moments I know she is near. As she said to me, "Death is like being in the next room."

Perhaps it's just wishful thinking. Maybe it's love. Or maybe it's something better. Maybe it's hope.

To learn more about *The Walk*
series or to join Richard's mailing list and
receive special offers and information please visit:
www.richardpaulevans.com

Join Richard on Facebook at the
Richard Paul Evans fan page
or *The Walk* **book series group.**

Or write to him at:
P.O. Box 712137 • Salt Lake City, Utah • 84171

*R*ichard Paul Evans is the #1 bestselling author of *The Christmas Box*. Each of his twenty novels has been a *New York Times* bestseller. There are more than fifteen million copies of his books in print worldwide, translated into more than twenty-four languages. He is the recipient of numerous awards, including the American Mothers Book Award, the *Romantic Times* Best Women's Novel of the Year Award, the German Audience Gold Award for Romance, two Religion Communicators Council Wilbur Awards, the *Washington Times* Humanitarian of the Century Award and the Volunteers of America National Empathy Award. He lives in Salt Lake City, Utah, with his wife, Keri, and their five children. You can learn more about Richard on Facebook at www.facebook.com/RPEfans, or visit his website, www.richardpaulevans.com.

SIMON & SCHUSTER
READING GROUP GUIDE

Introduction

Life is good for Alan Christoffersen. He has a beautiful wife, a great house, and is head of a growing company, but all at once, Alan's life changes permanently and irrevocably—he loses his family and job. Now completely on his own, Alan must figure out how to pick up the pieces and move on. He starts with a simple step, quite literally: he decides to go for a walk across America.

Discussion Questions

1. The author writes in the style of a diary. Do you enjoy this style of writing? Did it help you relate to the characters? Did you think it made the story stronger or weaker?

2. At the outset, Alan's life seems to be perfect. However, in the prologue he makes it clear things don't work out as he imagined. How did this admission and fore-shadowing affect your reading?

3. At the start of chapter three the author tells us "pro-crastination is the thief of dreams." Is this a true state-ment? How does that philosophy relate to Alan's life? Is it true in your life?

4. After McKale's accident, Alan is so preoccupied with her that his company disappears under his feet. What was his reaction to the news? How do you think you would have handled these major events all at once?

5. Alan became overwhelmed by his grief, yet he never lost his love for McKale. What does that say about him as a person and husband? How did those feelings help him through his pain?

6. Alan says he and McKale were each other's only

friends. Did this focus only on each other end up having a detrimental effect or positive one? Why?

7. Alan's father also lost his wife at an early age, and so had been through a similar situation. How did he support his son during the ordeal? Was it helpful?

8. The Christoffersens were terrible at handling money and quickly had all their belongings repossessed. How does this metaphor relate to what else Alan had lost?

9. Before almost killing himself, Alan heard a voice that said, "Life is not yours to take." Who, if anyone, was speaking to him, and what did that message mean?

10. Alan wrote in his diary he believed deep in our hearts we all want to walk free. Do you think that's true? Would people really prefer to be unchained from their belongings?

11. "A good walk in the woods is as effective as psychotherapy." What is Alan trying to gain from his walk? A chance to get away from his problems or a long therapy session or both?

12. At what point did you begin to see a change in Alan? Who do you feel had the most profound effect on him during his walk?

13. When McKale visits Alan in a vision, what did she mean when she talked about Angel? What relationship did she see between him and the woman whom

he helped on the highway? What relationship do you think Alan and Angel will have?

14. Where do you see the story headed? What other trials do you expect Alan to encounter on his way to Key West?

Enhance Your Book Club

1. Alan begins the story as a big shot ad executive. Create your own advertisement for *The Walk* and share it with the group. Explain how you created your design.

2. Alan spends much of the novel walking and thinking. Go for a walk with your group as you discuss the story.

3. Do you like to hike? Alan also became proficient in setting up tents and living off the land. Take a weekend trip to the woods or the mountains with your group to take in nature.

4. More than once Alan stopped in a restaurant claiming the best milkshakes in the world. What does it take to make the perfect shake? Create some with your group and see who can make the tastiest version.

A Conversation with Richard Paul Evans

1. What message are you trying to share with this novel?

I believe that we were meant to live as social creatures, to reach out and bless each other's lives. To paraphrase what Dickens wrote, ". . . it's required of all men to walk abroad among humanity."

2. Why did you decide to write in diary form, rather than another style?

I began writing in diary form nearly fifteen years ago with my second novel *Timepiece*. I enjoy doing it, and it makes for a very readable, interesting book.

3. There is a spiritual side to the novel as Alan wrestles with his feelings toward God. Why did you choose to add this aspect to the story?

It is my experience that almost everyone who suffers a major loss, whether a professed believer in God or not, wonders about God and struggles with either blame or confusion. It was an issue I wanted to address head-on, especially with Ally, the waitress, who asks: Why do we blame God for the bad things but not the good?

4. Are you like Alan, who said that everyone has a deep desire to leave everything behind and just keep moving? Or do you prefer to stay close to home?

Seeing I've been in thirteen cities in the last three weeks, I suppose I'm more like Alan than I want to believe. But as I get older, I long to just be home.

5. Why did you choose to call out certain parts of Alan's diary to start each chapter?

It's a style I've used before in my writing and one that is very popular with my readers. As I write, the focus is on creating a story that flows quickly, so the reader becomes lost in the experience. More prosaic passages can stop that flow. I discovered by pulling them out and putting them at the beginning of a chapter heading, where the reader is already transitioning, makes for a more enjoyable read.

6. You write a very descriptive narrative about Washington State where Alan travels and seem to have a lot of knowledge of the area. Have you traveled there before?

My daughter Jenna and I rented a car and drove the route, carefully observing what he would see, where he would stop, and what he would eat. I initially tried to write this story in my den and realized it was impossible to do without being there. This means that over the next four years, Jenna and I will travel across America together, something I'm very excited about.

7. Alan contemplates an important question on his walk that is good for you as well: Who really does have the greatest milkshakes?

I honestly don't know. I'm diabetic so I didn't try any. My daughter liked Zeke's.

8. *The Walk* is the first book in your planned series. What other adventures are in store for Alan on his trip?

You'll have to wait and see.

9. You've written a number of bestsellers. What is it about writing that you enjoy? What is your process in creating stories that people enjoy so much?

I suppose I have an active imagination and writing allows me to live it out. I truly feel as if I'm a conduit for these stories, and there are times that I don't even know what I'm writing until it's poured through me and I can confront it on the page. People are looking for inspiration, and my books are sometimes the vehicles of what people are looking for. It's my job, however, to make my books entertaining.

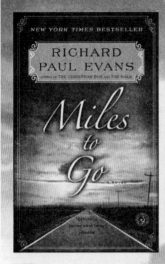
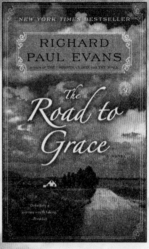